ᵃ**t."**

ardon?"

"I'm pregnant."

He waited.

"I just thought you should know." Phyllis Langford looked far too calm sitting there, her honey-colored purse, which matched her honey-colored shoes, still slung over her shoulder.

"I don't understand why I'm the one you're telling," he said carefully. He knew it wasn't polite to ask a woman who the father of her child was, but what did a guy say when it wasn't him? He might have lost a good piece of his mind that day, but not so much that he hadn't protected himself, and her, from any and all consequences.

"Because you're the only man I've had sex with since I divorced my husband four years ago." As he shook his head, she added softly, "Condoms fail."

"Not likely."

"Read the box the next time you pick some up," she said, still appearing far too calm. "Besides, when I thought about it, I realized the wrapper you took from your wallet didn't look exactly new."

Damn, the woman sounded as though they were discussing nothing more earth-shattering than a rained-out game of Little League. Didn't she get it? They had an untenable situation on their hands.

Matt didn't even know how to be a friend. There was no way he could be a father.

Dear Reader,

Have you ever found yourself disliked for something, some trait or skill, that's an integral part of you? Something you can't change? It's not an easy position to be in, but a very real one. To be a person deserving of happiness—a good person, a loving person—and yet alone. It was a situation that intrigued me, a situation I couldn't let go. I needed to know how such a thing could happen. To find the happy ending.

This is Phyllis Langford's story. If you've read any of my previous SHELTER VALLEY books, you'll remember her. *Just Around the Corner* is a story about the human spirit, about making the most of what life has given you, about enduring. And about happy endings. I believe there's a happy ending out there for everyone. It's just a matter of hanging on. Of not giving up. Eventually it will come knocking.

Each day of my life consists of hanging on, of not giving up—and of answering the door when I hear that knock. It doesn't come just once. It comes, for me, every day in one form or another. A phone call. A smile. A note. A hug.

I wish you all a lifetime of happy endings—and the ability to hear happiness knocking at your door when it arrives.

Tara Taylor Quinn

P.S. I love to hear from readers. Write me at P.O. Box 15065, Scottsdale, Arizona 85267-5065. Or visit my Web site at http://members.home.net/ttquinn.

SHELTER VALLEY STORIES

Just Around the Corner
Tara Taylor Quinn

TORONTO • NEW YORK • LONDON
AMSTERDAM • PARIS • SYDNEY • HAMBURG
STOCKHOLM • ATHENS • TOKYO • MILAN • MADRID
PRAGUE • WARSAW • BUDAPEST • AUCKLAND

ISBN 0-373-71027-5

JUST AROUND THE CORNER

For Tanya Elizabeth Clayton.
You, like Phyllis, are an amazing young woman.
I truly believe that you will take whatever life gives you
and make your own happy endings.
I'm very proud to be part of your life.

MOTHER
by Tanya Clayton

Every time you tell me something
That may help me
I turn the other way.
My pride says I won't listen
But my heart absorbs every word.
I always tell you I'll be a better mother
But I know I won't.
You have taught me lessons
That no one else could.
You have backed me up
When no one else would.
You have been my biggest fan
When everyone had given up.
You are my mother,
The person that I am part of
And the person I am proud of
Being part of every day.

CHAPTER ONE

THE KISS WAS as powerful as he was. As dangerous.

And beckoning.

Her arms crept around his neck, her lips pressing against his as excitement uncoiled in her belly. This was insane.

And she didn't want it to stop.

Phyllis had spent the entire day with Matt Sheffield. Seen him in action. And still knew absolutely nothing about him.

Because he wanted it that way.

Which made him even more desirable. Because she wanted it that way, too.

Dr. Phyllis Langford didn't need a man in her life—especially *this* man. Didn't need to know him, to get tangled up in the shadows she'd read in his eyes, the aloofness in his body.

What she needed was exactly what he was giving her. Lips that knew their destination, that didn't hesitate. Hands that touched her lonely body, igniting fires banked too long.

"We shouldn't be doing this," she said, her mind still engaged enough to recognize that much.

"Mm-hmm." The moan tingled against her lips.

His tongue penetrated her mouth, and Phyllis thrilled to his aggression. He felt so damn good. And it had been such a long time…. He placed her against the theater's sound-booth console in the performing-arts center at Montford University, where they'd spent the day working on a "Patterns of Abuse" presentation she'd be giving at a "Psychology In the University" seminar in that very theater later that month. The big window in front of them looked out over the dark and empty auditorium. The controls beneath them pushed into her back.

"Not here," he said suddenly, pulling her up and urging her toward the couch at the opposite end of the room.

The couch she'd been eyeing off and on all day, her mind filled with lascivious thoughts.

She'd just never dreamed her inappropriate and completely far-fetched fantasies would ever achieve reality there.

Hadn't really even decided she *wanted* them to.

His hands skimmed along her sides. Those same hands had been manipulating computer keys and technical equipment all afternoon. His lips left hers only long enough for breathing, and then they were consuming her again. Obliterating thought as he used his body to guide her on another erotic journey.

In spite of the sweet tension building inside her—the kind that made a woman forget she was a nice girl and allow anything as long as she found the satisfaction that was almost within reach—she might still have been able to stop him if he hadn't seemed as completely absorbed as she.

His hands weren't quite steady as they slid beneath her red chenille sweater. His breathing ragged, he kissed her chin, her neck and then was at her lips again.

Phyllis accommodated him. Lifting her mouth to his, she raised her body off the couch to let him slide her sweater up, exposing her belly. Her breasts ached for his touch, ached to be covered by those big capable hands. She arched against him.

God, she needed this. To feel desirable. To know she could drive a man to distraction. Maybe because losing the weight hadn't been enough to give her back the confidence she'd lost. Maybe because all her friends had this. Every single one of them was in love....

For a brief moment, as she lay there with her newly flat belly exposed, Phyllis panicked. Why had she thought of love now? She wasn't going to get involved again. Not like that. Not when hurt was inevitable.

And then she remembered. She wasn't in danger. Matt Sheffield wasn't the type to allow involvement.

Everyone in Shelter Valley respected his "hands off" signals. She'd only lived in the town a little more than a year—nothing like the four years he'd been the Fine Arts Technical Coordinator at Montford—yet she was much more a part of this community than he was. Other than the classes he taught, the events he oversaw, he kept to himself. He seemed to welcome neither personal conversation nor invitations. It didn't take a psychologist to figure out that the man was off-limits.

His lips burned her neck and then her belly, as his hands finally slid up over her breasts, cupping them, squeezing gently, the sensation excruciating in its intensity.

"Please," Phyllis was begging before she could stop herself.

"Please what?" he rasped.

"Please make love to me."

"I intend to, pretty woman." He took a condom out of his wallet before reaching for the button at the waistband of his jeans. "Believe me, I intend to."

He'd called her pretty.

They were the last coherent words Phyllis processed for a long time.

The next ones, uttered by her after silent, awkward moments of pulling on clothes that had been hastily discarded, were, "Well, goodbye."

"We used a condom." Phyllis looked across at her friend one Monday in the middle of October, her disbelief—and confusion—apparent.

Cassie Tate Montford, happily wearing maternity slacks and a blousy top as she entered her sixth month of pregnancy, looked as if she didn't know whether to smile or cry.

Phyllis didn't blame Cassie for her indecision. The two women had several things in common: their interest in pet therapy, their commitment to Shelter Valley...and their red hair. Now, apparently, they shared something else, as well.

Something Phyllis hadn't planned on at all.

"You're sure?" Cassie asked.

"I'm sure," Phyllis said, nodding her head, feeling more like a lost little girl than the Yale graduate she was.

They were in the sitting room at Montford Mansion, sharing cups of homemade hot chocolate, courtesy of Cassie's mother-in-law, Carol Montford. This was a rare moment of privacy for both of them. Mariah, Cassie and Sam's adopted daughter, was still at school. And Sam was at work, refurbishing homes, providing better-than-new living conditions for people who occupied the inadequate housing outside Shelter Valley. These places, built in the late 1890s, had fallen into disrepair as subsidized government housing, and Sam was renovating them at a reasonable cost to their current owners.

"So you're pregnant.... This might not be bad news, you know," Cassie said slowly, the tremulous smile seeming to win the battle of expressions on her beautiful face. "Babies are such blessings in so many ways. Raising a child is one of the greatest accomplishments possible. And you'll never be alone...."

Phyllis shook her head. "I'm not alone," she said, surprised by the sudden ache she felt at Cassie's pronouncement. "I have plenty of people to love. Plenty of people who love me."

Cassie was one of them.

"Of course you do," her friend said, her brow creased in a frown. "But no one who shares the ups and downs of daily life with you."

Phyllis couldn't argue with her there. She'd had that once, though. And in her case, being alone was the better option.

"I'm guessing you haven't told Matt."

Phyllis shook her head, her short, flyaway red curls the only vibrant thing about her.

"How do you think he's going to take the news?"

"Not well," Phyllis said, shrugging.

"Something, somewhere sucked all the love out of that man," Cassie said, her sweet brown eyes concerned. "He's been in town four years and has never—not once—accepted an invitation to anything. Not only does he always reject our hospitality, even at Christmas, but he's never attended any community function when he's not working. He was probably the only person in town who didn't attend the Fourth of July celebration last summer."

"I know," Phyllis said, wishing the chocolate that was warming her thick ceramic cup could warm her, too. "He's so...detached, and that's what made him so safe to begin with. I wanted sex, not involvement."

Cassie seemed to have more to say, but she sat there staring at Phyllis, instead. Phyllis could only wonder what her friend was thinking. And decided maybe she didn't want to know.

"It's not like he can be angry with me," Phyllis finally said. "It was *his* condom…."

"So you have every right to be angry with *him*."

Tilting her head, Phyllis grimaced. "And what good is that going to do me?"

"Give you the energy to cope," Cassie said with her customary frankness. The two women had worked together on more than one occasion, counseling abuse victims through Cassie's pet-therapy program, and they were used to speaking honestly. "Even negative energy is better than none at all."

Once again, Phyllis couldn't argue with her. Cassie had learned that particular truth the hard way, Phyllis knew, back when Cassie's entire life had fallen apart, and she'd disintegrated right along with it. She'd needed years to rebuild what she'd lost, to reshape her existence in a new form.

"I haven't even thought about coping yet," she admitted quietly.

Setting down her cup, Cassie said, "And I'm assuming you plan to have the baby when there's nothing that says you must."

"Of course I'm having it," Phyllis said, running her finger along the outer seam of her jeans. "You know me well enough to know that. I only found out this morning, so it's not like I've had time to make a single plan, but *not* having this baby isn't even a choice for me.''

"You want it," Cassie guessed, her brown eyes piercing.

Looking up at her friend, Phyllis smiled. "I guess I do.''

Cassie lifted her cup and sipped carefully from her chocolate. "So,'' she said, leaning forward on the couch, her legs spread slightly to accommodate her growing belly. "What kind of cooperation are you hoping to get from Matt Sheffield?''

"Not marriage, that's for sure,'' Phyllis said. That would naturally be one of the first assumptions people would make, but she wasn't even going to consider it.

"While I have to admit I'm relieved that you aren't holding out hope that the man's going to do the right thing by you, do you have to be quite so adamant about being better off single?''

They'd had this discussion before. Phyllis understood that with Cassie's newfound happiness, and her current state of being head over heels in love, she wanted the same satisfaction for those she cared about. Phyllis got that satisfaction in other ways, but she knew better than to argue with Cassie.

"Financially you'll be okay, even if he denies all responsibility?'' Cassie asked.

"Okay, and then some.''

Elbows on her knees, Cassie rested her chin in her hands, staring down at her bare feet, and then over at the fashionable ankle boots Phyllis was wearing with her size-six jeans.

"You really look great, you know that?"

The words brought a smile to Phyllis's face. "Thanks." But then the expression faded as something else hit her. "I've lost forty pounds, I'm finally feeling positive about myself, and now I'm going to turn around and get fat again."

"But only for a while," Cassie reminded her. "And for a very good cause." She cradled her own belly, obviously loving every pound, every outward sign that she was truly carrying a baby of her own. She'd been told years ago, after the death of her first born, that she'd never conceive a child again.

"Yeah." Phyllis nodded, still a bit concerned. Those pounds of hers had not come off easily. Through many long months of struggle, she'd promised herself that she'd never see them again.

"Did you read *Borough Bantam* this week?" Cassie asked suddenly. As a diversion, the tactic was a little rough around the edges, but Phyllis was eager to turn her thoughts away from her own situation, if only for a minute or two. She nodded.

"The little mouse character picked out a boy's name and a girl's name in case a new mouse comes to live with her. You've obviously been talking to Mariah about the baby."

Borough Bantam was a nationally syndicated

comic strip depicting a village of creatures who, through their daily and often comical adventures, imparted gentle lessons and observations about life. Cassie's husband, Sam, the creator, had fashioned them after people he'd grown up with in Shelter Valley, his way of keeping in touch with his home and everything he'd left behind during his ten-year exile from the place he loved. The little mouse in the strip represented Mariah, the little girl Sam had adopted when her parents, his best friends, had been killed by terrorists on the other side of the world.

"We have." Cassie's smile was tinged with sadness. "She's insisting we name the baby either Brian or Morning Glory."

"After her parents?"

"Yeah. Her mother's name was Moira, but Mariah always says Morning."

"So are you and Sam going to keep those names?"

"Absolutely. How can we not? Our daughter speaks her mind, we listen."

For the first few months Mariah had lived with Sam, she'd been mute, a result of the trauma of witnessing her parents' death. Cassie and her pet therapy had been the way by which Mariah was able to heal. It was also the way Cassie and Sam found each other again.

"So is Sam used to everyone in town thinking he's a hero for creating *Bantam?*" Phyllis asked. She knew that Cassie's husband had been more than a little worried about his reception—and that of his comic strip—when he'd returned to town after so many years.

"I don't know if he'll ever get used to it," Cassie said honestly. "He was so sure they'd think he was poking fun at them and hate him for it. But I think he's getting just a bit tired of everyone trying to help him write it!"

"They all have ideas, huh?" Phyllis commiserated, and Cassie nodded.

"So, back to Sheffield," Cassie said. "What are your expectations?"

Shaking her head, Phyllis set her cup farther from the edge of the end table. "I'm expecting nothing from him," she said. "Our being together—it just...happened. Wasn't planned. Other than when we put on the psychology seminar last week, we haven't spoken."

Cassie studied her friend. "And you were happy about that."

"Absolutely."

"And now?"

"Now I'm just trying to deal with the ramifications of this pregnancy in my own life. Matt Sheffield doesn't matter to me at all."

Sighing, seeming oddly relieved, Cassie sat back. "Can I tell you something then?"

"Of course."

"If Matt reacts coldly to the news, don't take it

personally. I don't think the man's capable of softer feelings.''

Phyllis frowned. ''Why do you say that?''

''Last year I had a litter of pups that'd been left at the clinic,'' Cassie said. ''I took them down to campus one afternoon, offering them to anyone who might want a dog. While I was busy giving care instructions for one of them, another puppy got tangled up in one of the leashes I'd brought along with the stuff I was giving away to the new owners. Sheffield walked by and didn't even stop. He just left that puppy there, squirming and frightened.''

''Maybe he didn't see it.''

''He saw it,'' Cassie assured her. ''He looked right at us. Besides, when he walked by, the puppy started to squeal, which is what alerted me to the whole thing.''

Shrugging, Phyllis looked tired as she laid her head back against the chair. ''So maybe he doesn't like dogs. Probably got bitten by one as a kid.''

''Spoken like a true psychologist. Always looking for the hidden motivations.''

''Everybody has them.''

''Maybe he's just incapable of caring for anything or anyone,'' Cassie said softly.

''Maybe.''

Phyllis didn't care one way or the other.

''You know,'' Cassie said, leaning forward to lay a hand on Phyllis's arm. ''Between Tory and me and Becca and everyone else in Shelter Valley who's fallen in love with you, we'll get you through this pregnancy. And we'll give you whatever help you need for the next eighteen years or more of single motherhood. No sweat. You can count on that.''

Phyllis's eyes filled. ''Thank you.''

''What we can't do,'' Cassie said, her voice taking on a note of warning, ''is prevent—or cure—a broken heart.''

Nodding, Phyllis believed her friend. Cassie should know. She'd lived with one for more than ten years. And from the sound of things, there'd been days when the pain had been almost enough to kill her.

''Don't worry,'' she said, ''this heart is firmly intact.'' *And going to remain that way.*

As DAYS WENT, it wasn't a good one. Matt Sheffield wondered what he'd done to piss off the fates *this* time. The new gels had come in for the dance show that weekend and they were the wrong colors. The light board—the computer that controlled the lighting—had crashed, so the lights weren't working. He had a student working for him who could only be described as technically challenged, the kids in his lighting design class had all acted as though they'd rather be someplace else, and his star student, Sophie Curtis, had been missing cues all morning.

And it was a dance show. His least-favorite kind of production to entrust to students. Plays were usually easy to light—a wash, some specials—unless they were going for extravagant effects. Concerts were even easier, symposiums downright boring. But dance—now there, the lighting was part of the art. He could lose himself in creativity and forget about life for a while.

Unless he had butts to wipe every step of the way.

And Sophie...she'd been preoccupied all semester. In the two years he'd known her, Sophie had done nothing but amaze him, with her diligence, her reliability, but mostly her vision. She could make magic out of an empty stage with almost nothing. Whether she was working as lighting designer, stage manager or sound engineer, she was always the glue that held the rest of the students together.

Until this semester. She'd been late, absent-minded, short-tempered. She'd lost weight.

Something was wrong.

Not that Matt had any intention of finding out what.

"You busy?"

He glanced up from his desk in the office at the back of the performing-arts center to see who actually had the nerve to interrupt his lunch hour—the one time he could let down his guard and allow free rein to whatever thoughts he felt like having.

Dr. Phyllis Langford was standing there. The psych professor. Matt's stomach dropped at about the same rate his heart sped up.

The day just kept getting better and better. Not.

"Finishing my lunch," he said, indicating the

empty sandwich wrapper on the desk in front of him. He wadded up the debris, put it and the empty chip bag in the little brown sack he'd brought from home and lobbed the whole package into the trash can beside his desk.

"I knew you had class this afternoon and I wanted to catch you before you went in."

She hadn't come any farther into the room. Just stood there, not quite meeting his eyes, but not looking around at anything else, either. An odd mixture of confidence and disinterest. Funny, the month before, he'd only noticed the confidence.

Confidence and passion and... *No.* They'd forgotten that insane lapse in the production room. They were both going to ignore it, both going to act as though it had never happened.

He studied her through narrowed eyes, hoping they had indeed forgotten. He'd sweated for a couple of days after their tumble that afternoon, afraid she'd come calling with expectations he'd never meet.

And had been honestly, greatly relieved—despite a slightly damaged ego—that she hadn't. Apparently he'd lost his touch with women; under the circumstances, that was nothing but a blessing.

"You can come in," he said when she continued to hover. He didn't want her anywhere near him or his office, but she was making him edgy, just standing there silently full of something to say.

That same sexy scent—the one that had lured him to insanity last month—drifted in with her as she took a seat on the other side of his desk. Phyllis Langford didn't perch on the edge of her chair as many women did—at least in his office. There was nothing tentative or uncertain in the way she sat, somehow commanding the space around her with her model-slim body. She'd had on black lycra bell-bottom pants the day he'd spent with her. Today she was wearing a circumspect, honey-colored business suit.

He wasn't sure which he found sexier.

"I'm pregnant."

Matt blinked. Froze inside. *"Pardon?"*

"I'm pregnant."

He waited.

"I just thought you should know." Dr. Langford, as he preferred to think of her, looked far too calm sitting there, her honey-colored purse, which matched her honey-colored shoes, still slung over her shoulder.

Her hair, a red version of Meg Ryan's stylishly messy do, distracted him.

"I don't understand why I'm the one you're telling," he said carefully, studying that hair. He knew it wasn't polite to ask a woman who the father of her child was, but what did a guy say when it wasn't him? He might have lost a good piece of his mind that Saturday in the theater, but not so much that he hadn't protected himself, and her, from any and all consequences.

"Because you're the only man I've had sex with since I divorced my husband four years ago."

He shook his head, not thinking her a liar, just knowing his stuff. "I pulled on that condom before I got anywhere near you."

"Condoms fail."

"Not likely."

"Read the box next time you pick some up," she said, still appearing far too calm, too undemanding, to be telling him what he thought he was hearing. "They're ninety-seven percent safe. Which leaves three percent for us to fall into."

No.

"Added to the fact that, once I thought back on it, I realized the wrapper you took from your wallet didn't look exactly new."

It hadn't been. But the damn things didn't come with "use by" dates. For a reason.

"How long was it in there?" she asked.

He shrugged, uncomfortable. His private life was off-limits. Period.

Or it had been until last month, when he'd pulled down the zipper on the front of his jeans in the Performing Arts Center. Every swearword he could think of—his time in prison had given him quite a repertoire—passed through his mind. Attached to each one was a barb aimed directly at the guilty part of his anatomy.

"I don't know," he finally said. "A year, maybe more."

Like, maybe three more. It'd been a long, long time since he'd relaxed enough to give in to a sexual urge.

"A year's worth of being smooshed and sat on could definitely do it," she said.

Damn, the woman sounded as though they were discussing nothing more earth-shattering than a rained-out game of Little League. Didn't she get it? They had an untenable situation on their hands.

Matt didn't even know how to be a friend. There was no way he could be a father.

"I…" He paused, wondering what to say to her, to make her understand.

"Don't worry." She jumped into the pause. "I'm not asking anything from you. I don't *want* anything. What happened last month was a one-time, no-strings-attached episode. And that hasn't changed."

Episode. They'd had some of the most incredible sex of his life. They'd apparently made a baby. And she called it an episode?

Was that all the baby was to her, too? An episode? Easy come, easy go? The thought made him feel a little sick.

He opened his mouth to tell her so.

Whoa. He stopped just in time.

A few minutes ago he'd been looking for a way to bail. He could hardly blame her, a single woman with a prominent position at a prestigious college, for wanting to do the same.

Admittedly, bailing was a little more convenient for him than it would be for her.

"Do you mind if I ask what your plans are?" He'd pay whatever expenses she incurred. Money was the one thing he had to give.

For the first time since taking a seat, she looked down, and he saw the chink in her armor. Was oddly relieved to find it there.

"I haven't really made any plans yet," she told him. "I'm still getting used to the idea that I'm going to be a mother."

Going to be a mother. Why did his mind keep repeating everything she said? You'd think he was dense or something.

"You're planning to have the baby, then?"

Her head shot back up. "Of course. And before you ask, I'm not even considering the alternative, so you can save your breath."

"I wasn't going to ask."

CHAPTER TWO

IT WAS GOING much better than she'd expected. And worse. She'd prepared herself for anger, denial, blame.

What she hadn't prepared for was a thoughtful, concerned man. Inexplicably, his humanness made the whole thing so much harder to get through. He was supposed to be little more than a fly at her picnic. She'd swat him away and get on with it.

He wasn't letting that happen—wasn't letting her discount him as easily as she'd thought.

"So you're definitely going to have the baby." He was fooling with a paper clip on his desk. Bending it into odd shapes with two fingers of his left hand. Did that mean he was left-handed? She hadn't noticed before.

Did that mean her baby might be left-handed, as well?

"Yes, I'm going to have it." She swallowed. Her baby. And this man's.

He looked up, head cocked to one side, eyes narrowed. "I can't be a father."

The sigh of relief escaped Phyllis before she could prevent it. "Who asked you to be?"

Back to his paper clip. She wondered if he was staring at it so intently because he was really trying to create some particular design—or because he didn't want to look at her.

"I'll pay for everything."

"That won't be necessary."

A baby. A baby with her traits and his, all mixed together. Growing inside her body.

He raised his head, frowning. "Of course it's necessary. I'm responsible. I pay."

Two could play that game. "I'm responsible. I pay."

"Well, then, we're both responsible. We split the bills fifty-fifty."

No! That wasn't the plan. She was doing this alone.

But he had her. They *were* both responsible. She just hadn't figured he'd care. How was she to know he had a streak of responsibility in his reclusive body?

"Have you been to the doctor yet?"

Phyllis shook her head. *Don't do this,* she silently begged him. *Don't confuse me. Don't weaken me by carrying any of my load, or I might not be able to carry it all when you walk away.*

"You'll let me know when your appointment is?"

She couldn't breathe. Needed to get outside, let the cool October air chill her skin. Remind herself that she was okay.

"Why?" Somehow her voice sounded almost normal.

He shrugged. "I'm half-responsible. I should know stuff like that."

"Just how much are you counting on here? What exactly will you want to know?"

"Not sure." He'd picked up another paper clip. This one with his right hand. "I'm new at this, too. I guess when something costs money, I should know about it."

That wasn't as bad as she'd begun to think. It wasn't personal. Merely financial.

"I'll see that you get copies of the bills."

His face expressionless, he nodded.

"There's one other thing," she added quickly.

Matt looked up at her, his eyes wary, questioning.

"Cassie Montford knows you're the father—it seemed necessary that *someone* know in case something happens—but she's been sworn to secrecy. I don't want anyone else knowing."

He seemed to consider that for several moments. "It would probably make things easier on both of us," he said at last.

Phyllis stood, satisfied. "That's what I thought."

"Good."

"Good."

"Well, send me the bills." Tossing the paper clip, he stood, too.

"I will."

"Okay, see ya." He'd followed her to the door.

"Goodbye." Phyllis spoke with finality.

If she had her way, they'd never see each other again.

He made her tremble. He made her crazy and just a little angry. She absolutely refused to let him become part of her life.

She didn't want or need his financial contributions.

This time it was the bills and not the check that would get mysteriously lost in the mail.

THE KICKING BAG went down. And came back up. Then went down again. Turning, Matt caught it with a perfectly placed side kick, knocking it into the corner of the wall. And, with hands properly angled in front of him, he turned and landed another perfect blow with the opposite foot.

Sweat dripped down the sides of his face. He didn't bother wiping it off. It burned his eyes, but he ignored the pain, which was only the minutest portion of the punishment he deserved.

After more than an hour in his home gym, he wasn't even close to the worn-out state he was working toward.

How could he have done it? He of all people?

Had life taught him nothing? The time he'd never be able to recapture. The humiliation and abuse. The lost dreams. Lost innocence. Had it all been for nothing?

Another smack on the bag, and the sand-weighted bottom scooted along the floor.

He just couldn't believe what was happening. Couldn't have imagined a worse day than the one he'd just had.

He'd made a woman pregnant. A perfectly respectable doctor of psychology was facing a complete and permanent upheaval in her life because of him.

Forgetting himself to the point of lost discipline, Matt hauled off and slugged the kicking bag with both fists, over and over, like a novice and completely unskilled boxer, rather than the Tae Kwon Do black belt he was. Logically he knew he was solving nothing. That he was probably going to hurt himself.

But he couldn't stop. Couldn't harness the anger, the despair and disappointment coursing through him. Didn't know what to do next, except wear himself out, force himself into complete exhaustion. How was he going to live with himself?

He'd just begun to find a measure of internal peace. Maybe even forgiveness. And in the span of a ten-minute office visit, years of hard work, of unrelenting self-control and mental promises, had been shot to hell.

He'd been in Shelter Valley for four years. Pretending to himself that he was building a new life, becoming the man he'd always expected himself to be.

When instead, he was exactly what he'd been before Will Parsons had been kind enough to give him this job, this chance.

A man who'd spent years in prison. He hadn't been guilty of the statutory rape of which he'd been convicted. But he hadn't been entirely blameless, either. He'd allowed that girl—a student—to think he found her desirable. He hadn't intended to; he'd only meant to offer a confused young girl a measure of confidence, a sense of approval. In his own idealistic ignorance, he'd tried to help someone and had only confused her more.

Slumping to the carpet, sweat dripping down his back and chest beneath the soaked T-shirt he was wearing, Matt grabbed his aching head between both fists.

The tears, when they dripped slowly from beneath tightly closed lids, mixed in with the sweat. Fell unnoticed. Forgotten. Allowing no forgiveness for a sin not committed—and then committed six years after the fact.

This was the second time he'd contributed to the ruin of a perfectly lovely woman's life.

He deserved to rot in hell.

And that was just what he feared would happen to him. Only it would be a hell of his own making, right here on earth, in this place of shelter where everyone else had family and friends and knew the comforts afforded by love. It was going to be his own private hell. Even in this journey of everlasting destruction, he would be all alone.

IT WAS LATE on the first Tuesday night in November, and Phyllis had just arrived home from Phoenix when the phone rang. She'd been at a pet-therapy session with Cassie and a woman who'd been brutally raped by a colleague while working in a nursing home.

Sighing, she picked up the phone, a portable. "Surely you've seen a doctor by now." The voice didn't bother with introductions or hellos.

She considered lying, but that wasn't her style.

"I have."

"When? Today? Is that where you've been all evening?"

If he'd sounded like someone who was checking up on her—instead of like someone who was driving himself crazy with frustration—Phyllis would've been able to handle the conversation a lot more effectively.

"I went last week," she admitted. "Today I've been in Phoenix with Cassie Montford, helping her with her pet therapy. We went to see a woman in Phoenix who's crawled so deeply inside herself that she'll respond to nothing but one of Cassie's dogs. We're using the dog Angel to help her learn how to trust enough to interact with human beings again. If we don't succeed, she's going to live the rest of her life shut away in an institution."

Phyllis wasn't usually a babbler, but it didn't take a genius to figure out that she didn't want to give Matt a chance to say what he'd called to say. She'd managed to put him out of her mind for hours at a time this past week. She didn't need him back there.

"Have you had any success?" he asked when her words finally stopped.

Sinking into the couch in her tiny living room, Phyllis leaned back and stared at the ceiling. "Yeah, just tonight," she told him, feeling strangely comforted.

Cassie had Sam at home, waiting to hear all about it. Phyllis had no one.

"She's been petting Angel for weeks without reacting at all. Tonight, for the first time, she looked at her and there were tears in her eyes."

"And that's good?"

"It means she's in there—and that she's starting to come out. She's going to need a whole lot of reassurance before that can happen, though."

"She didn't cry before?"

Phyllis said no, started a technical explanation of hysterical amnesia and paralysis, and her own understanding of the things she'd read in the abused woman's eyes, and then abruptly stopped herself. She'd learned long ago that people didn't want to hear any of these things. She must be more tired than she'd thought.

"And you could tell she was searching for reassurance just from that one look at a dog?" he asked.

"Yeah," Phyllis said softly. "Her mind's been protecting her for a long time. She's lived inside a place that exists only in her own head, and she's afraid to come out. She's going to need constant reassurance that when she does, there's a safe, protected environment waiting for her."

"And you can provide that in weekly visits?"

"Of course not." Kicking off her shoes, Phyllis pulled her feet onto the sofa, tucking them beneath her. "We're just the door through which she's going to travel. The environment is right there waiting for her. She has a team of counselors working with her. People who've been around her, speaking with her, for months. At least one of them is with her twenty-four hours a day."

"What about her family? Do they come to see her?"

"Her sister does. Everyday. The two of them lived together before Ella was raped."

"Isn't it hard sometimes? Dealing with stuff like this?" He asked a question Phyllis rarely allowed herself to ask. "Seems like it could be...painful."

"It is," Phyllis said, remembering the year before, when she'd had Tory Sanders living with her. Under her guidance, Tory had been coming to terms with her abusive past, as well as grieving for her dead sister—Phyllis's best friend, Christine. "But then the light goes on in someone's eyes and suddenly I have all the energy in the world," she continued. "I've learned that when I'm feeling discouraged about a patient's recovery, I need to focus on the eventual appearance of that light, to look for it in the tiniest of signs, and I find myself getting little bursts of energy."

"Like tonight."

"Right."

"You're amazing." There was wonderment in his tone, and Phyllis felt an impulse, irrational but overpowering, to dismiss Matt's approval.

"I also spend most of my working hours in a classroom lecturing to healthy students," she reminded him. "Cases like this happen much less frequently."

"So what did the doctor have to say?"

She stiffened. He'd caught her off guard. Again.

"To take my vitamins."

"Everything's okay?"

He wasn't supposed to ask. Or care.

"Yes."

"I don't think I saw a bill. An insurance deductible, maybe? Vitamins?"

They both knew he hadn't.

Sitting up, Phyllis slipped back into her shoes and walked to her bedroom. She was tired. Needed a long soak in a hot tub. Just as soon as she got him off the phone.

"I'm a psychologist, Matt. I know about emotions and relationships, and I'm very sure that this will be much healthier for both of us if we agree to let this situation be mine."

"I—"

"I don't need your help. Not financially or in any other way," she interrupted, lining up her shoes in her closet. She'd been doing this ever since she'd seen her friend Randi do it. Now her shoes were much easier to find. Besides, she found the effect visually pleasing—and any activity that created a sense of order was a good thing, in her view. "As a matter-of-fact, if you want to help me, then rest assured that what would help the most is if you'd just let me get on with my life. There's no point including you when neither of us want you to be part of either my life or this child's."

"But—"

"I promise to call you if anything changes," she said. "If I get into trouble or have any problems, I won't hesitate to let you know."

"You'd better mean that," he said, his voice rougher then usual.

"I do."

"Then I guess I'll be seeing you."

Not if she could avoid it.

The man confounded her. He jumbled her thoughts—and that was something Phyllis just could not tolerate. Her emotions she couldn't always dictate, but her mind was the one thing she had to be able to count on. And Matt Sheffield threatened her mental clarity, her ability to analyze, to make rational, informed decisions. She hung up the phone with finality.

"Okay, baby," she said, her voice several notches higher—and happier—as she bent to run her bath. "Let's go play in the tub and then I'll give you a nice long rubdown with the oil the doctor gave us. How does that sound?"

It was still far too early in her pregnancy for any response from the tiny fetus growing inside her, but Phyllis knew that somehow the baby heard her and was learning to recognize his mother's voice.

That might not be a rational belief—more of an intuitive conviction—but Phyllis didn't question it for a second.

MATT HAD NO REASON to be at the faculty meeting. He rarely attended them, preferring to have pressing business at the theater whenever Will Parsons called a meeting with his faculty and staff.

Will had never given him any crap about his inclination to steer clear of large groups—a bit of leftover discomfort from the claustrophobia he'd developed in prison. But he'd always made certain that Matt received whatever information he needed.

Matt suspected that the older man understood the more urgent reason he chose to keep his distance from his colleagues. The more time Matt spent in their company, the more chance they'd ask the kinds of personal questions he didn't want to answer.

He caught Will's raised eyebrow when he slipped into the back of the large lecture hall, where the university president was giving his mid-November faculty address.

If Matt wasn't careful, he was going to be raising other questions he wasn't prepared to answer.

He noticed Phyllis Langford sitting between an English professor and the head of the Psych Department, up near the front of the hall, and slid into the back corner seat. She was the reason he was there, the person he needed to speak to. He had no concrete ideas of what he was going to say to her, no suggestions to present. He only knew that, through her, he had to find some degree of absolution. He had to reach an understanding of his role in this whole baby thing, otherwise he'd never get rid of the guilt.

Will announced all the shows scheduled at the Performing Arts Center during the holidays. Mentally planning his crews, Matt felt a twinge of unease as Sophie Curtis topped the list on every show that mattered. As stage manager of the most recent show she'd worked, the girl had missed several cues, failed to get the props onstage in time, pulled the curtain too soon and left the house lights lowered for the first five minutes of intermission.

Matt couldn't remember when he'd last seen her smile. She barely resembled the vivacious blonde of a year ago.

Will Parsons was speaking about a new promotional video the college was making. Matt would help with the shooting of some of the inside segments—and probably have a hand in the editing process, as well. He'd designed a couple of gobos—metal pieces placed in front of lights to throw shadows for special effect—they'd be using.

He was still finishing a note to himself when the meeting ended and his co-workers started filing past. A few nodded at him politely. The dance director smiled. No one stopped to speak.

He relaxed a bit.

And waited.

Phyllis Langford walked right past him, engrossed in conversation with her department head. She was wearing a navy suit today, with a navy-and-white polka-dot blouse. She looked great.

And not the least bit pregnant.

"Hi," he said, stepping up behind her.

Swinging around, she knocked into him, her purse walloping him in the ribs. "Matt! Hi," she said, smiling at him for a second. He hated how quickly her face sobered. "Did you need something?" she asked much more hesitantly, glancing at her superior.

Matt glanced at the older man, as well, wondering if Phyllis had any interest in him other than a professional one.

Wondering, too, if *his* baby was going to prevent her from pursuing that interest.

"I'd like to see you for a second, if you've got the time," he said. She was the entire reason he was at the damn Friday-afternoon meeting. A carefully planned, casual running into each other, just to see how she was doing. He hadn't spoken with her in almost two weeks.

Excusing herself to Dr. Ellington, Phyllis followed Matt out into the hall.

"What's up?" She appeared to be very carefully keeping a distance between them as they walked out of the building and across campus toward the faculty lot where they'd both parked. Matt was grateful to her for that distance.

"Just wanted to make sure there were no problems."

She frowned. "I told you I'd call if there were."

"I know."

"So?"

"I'm just making sure."

"Matt, the whole idea is that I'm on my own here. That means you don't check up on me."

He nodded. Glad to hear she still seemed confident in her decision. And then he remembered the good Dr. Ellington.

"Have dinner with me this weekend," he said before he could weigh the consequences of his words.

"No."

"We can go to Phoenix, someplace no one we know will see us together." Her refusal made him more determined. He was doing this for her. And for him, too, he guessed. Somehow he had to find a way to live with himself. He couldn't allow the pregnancy to throw her whole social life, her career plans, off course.

"No."

"I have something to discuss with you," he said, thinking of ways she could have his child and still date and attend conferences and do all the things she'd done before. He hadn't thought of one, but maybe together they could come up with something....

"What?"

There was no way she could be pregnant with his child and continue with her life as it had been. He just had to accept that fact—and accept his share of the blame.

"My family medical history," he said, coming up with the idea at the last minute. "You should know my medical background. Your doctor should have it."

"She did ask..." Phyllis said, and then stopped. Stopped speaking. Stopped walking. She looked up at Matt, her eyes serious, her lips firm.

"All right, one dinner, but that's all," she said. "And then I'm on my own."

"Agreed."

Matt meant what he said. But he didn't feel good about it.

CHAPTER THREE

THINKING IT WOULD BE easier to talk if they weren't facing each other across a table the entire time, Matt suggested he and Phyllis drive up to Tortilla Flat on Saturday, have a late lunch there, and then return to Shelter Valley. That gave them about five hours to reach some kind of accord.

And then get out of each other's lives.

Phyllis surprised him by agreeing immediately to the date that wasn't a date.

Things were awkward at first as she climbed into his Blazer late Saturday morning and they headed out. She was wearing a pair of designer-looking jeans and a thick black velour sweater that only accentuated the slimness of her small-boned frame.

It had been so long since he'd been out with anyone for any kind of social occasion that he'd more or less forgotten how to do it.

"It's a little disturbing to think that we made a baby and know so little about each other, huh?" She broke the awkward silence, apparently reading his mind.

It was disconcerting how she always seemed to know just what to say to get him started. She'd done that in his office the day she'd come to tell him about the pregnancy. And then again on the phone. Hell, she'd probably done it that day they'd worked together in the Performing Arts Center; he'd just been too busy listening to his libido to hear.

He was going to be damn glad when this day was over and he could go back to being the only one privy to the thoughts of Matt Sheffield.

"So how long have you been a professor?" he asked, taking her comment as a cue.

"Eight years, though I didn't start out with a full professorship."

"You like it?" Matt turned the utility vehicle onto the highway that led to Phoenix and beyond.

"I love it," she said, staring out at the road. He caught a glimpse of the smile on her face as he glanced over.

"Me, too," he said. They had something in common. He didn't know if that made the job ahead of them easier—or not.

She turned her head to look at him. "How long have you been teaching?"

This was why he avoided social occasions. And relationships. The questions inevitably led to places that were off-limits.

"Twelve years, on and off."

"Always at a college level?"

He shook his head, reluctant to remember. "I started out teaching theater technology to junior-high and high-school students."

"You said you've been teaching on and off. What did you do in the off parts?"

"Went to school, for one." Matt ran his hand underneath the collar of his open black leather jacket. He wished he could shove a towel down his back to soak up the sweat collecting there. "Got my masters in theater technology with an emphasis on lighting design. I also graduated from a certificate program in videography."

Relieved when there were no further questions, Matt concentrated on getting them through Phoenix and onto the two-lane, winding road that would take them up to Tortilla Flat. Apache Trail, as it had been dubbed more than a hundred years before, was at one time the only wagon trail going up to this part of northern Arizona. Tortilla Flat, though only ten miles up the mountain, was about a forty-five-minute drive. It had been the first stagecoach stopping place on the three-day journey from Phoenix to Roosevelt Dam.

The town, now more a tourist spot than anything, was reminiscent of those days, with most of the six or so buildings preserved in their original state. With its population of six, the town boasted a small store and ice-cream shop, a post office and well-known restaurant-cum-gift shop. The businesses were all run by the six-member family that resided there.

"I've never been up here." Phyllis broke the silence that had fallen around them, a silence that seemed so persistent Matt had begun to wonder if they'd actually get around to discussing anything that day.

He'd almost convinced himself that he hoped not.

"This scenery is beautiful," she continued.

Matt glanced around at the cacti and rocks, the dark greens and myriad shades of brown, the mountains rising above him on one side, the mile-long canyon on the other.

"I come up here fairly regularly," he admitted. Especially when he was feeling his worst. The vast miles of deserted landscape always seemed to put things in perspective for him. Reminded him just how small he was—or just how big the picture.

She turned to look at him, making him uncomfortable. Somehow he'd let too much show again.

"So tell me about your family," she said as he maneuvered slowly around the curves with their huge drop-offs only a foot away. There was no guardrail between them and those canyons.

Usually Matt liked the sense of danger he felt whenever he drove here. Today he was too aware of the woman beside him—and the baby growing inside her.

"Not much to tell," he said eventually, shrugging, rubbing a sweaty hand along the leg of his jeans before returning it to the wheel.

"You said you had family history to give me," she reminded him. "It's why I'm here."

He nodded. Took another curve. "Basically we

were all healthy,'' he said, trying to remember without thinking back.

''We?'' she asked. She'd turned again, had drawn up one knee as she faced him. ''How many of you were there?''

''Just my brother and sister and me. And my mother and father, of course.'' You couldn't forget them.

''No predisposition to any diseases that you know of? Nothing genetic we need to worry about?''

Matt froze. Nothing. At least not the kind of thing she was referring to. What she *wasn't* asking and needed to know about was a different predisposition altogether—the tendency to get oneself thrown in jail that seemed to beset the male Sheffields. There were some basic values missing in the men of his family.

There was a time Matt had believed he'd been spared that particular curse. A time he'd convinced himself that if he *did* have it, he'd gotten the better of it, risen above it.

He'd been full of shit back then.

''My mother was anemic after she had me and my sister, but that was all.''

''Any cancer you're aware of?''

''None.''

''Are they all still alive?''

How the hell did he answer that? Glancing over at her, Matt saw the warm interest in her intent green eyes—interest that, regardless of the magnificent scenery, was reserved for him.

It was inevitable that she'd find out. He owed her the chance to raise her kid right in spite of the strikes against him.

''I don't know,'' he said slowly.

He glanced over once more—in time to see the look of surprise that she quickly masked—and then he kept his eyes firmly on the hairpin turns in front of him. There was little traffic on the road, except for the occasional car approaching from the opposite direction.

And some motorcycles he could see in the distance behind him.

He waited for her to say something. For the questions to start. Nothing happened.

The turns kept coming. He continued, somehow, to stay on the road as he tackled them.

''My father died when I was in high school.'' Murdered in prison because he'd accosted one too many of the new arrivals. He'd found one who'd managed to smuggle in a weapon.

''I'm sorry.''

She sounded so sincere he almost looked over at her again. But he knew better. Matt Sheffield needed sympathy—caring—from no one. That was his golden rule.

One that had served him well.

''Don't be,'' he said. There was no need for her to waste her sympathy. ''We weren't close.''

''You didn't live together?''

''Off and on.''

"Your parents were divorced, then?"

"No."

"You want to tell me about it?"

"No."

"Do I need to know?"

Probably.

Another turn. And a car passing on the left. Matt slowed down from twenty miles an hour to a crawl.

"The first thing I remember about my father happened when I was about two. The cops came to our door and put handcuffs on him and hauled him away. He wasn't back the next morning."

He paused. Waited for her reaction—disgust, contempt, horror. Or maybe pity. The reactions, though varied in strength, were basically all the same.

Phyllis held hers in.

"That was only the first arrest. There were many more." He paused. "I don't know how old I was when I realized what my mom did while he was gone—the different men friends she ran around with, the bars. Trying to find forgetfulness, I guess."

At least that was the justification he'd created for her. The one he could stomach.

"And love," Phyllis said quietly.

"If that's what she wanted, she wasn't looking in the right places."

"Not everyone is as smart as you."

He replayed the words a couple of times, searching for the sarcasm. He found only open understanding. From a woman who didn't know him at all.

A woman who'd spent only one day with him. A day that had resulted in irrevocable consequences. The baby. He couldn't forget, even for a moment, about his most recent fall from grace.

"Every time my father went to jail, he was gone for a longer period. The last time, he never made it back home."

"He died in prison."

"Not from a disease. You don't have to worry about that," he assured her, coming up to a one-way bridge. He waited for the approaching car to go first. "He was murdered."

Stepping lightly on the gas, Matt guided the Blazer over the bridge.

"And your mother?"

"She ran off with her boyfriend."

"And abandoned you and your brother and sister?"

"Just me. My brother was...gone by then. And she took my sister. Lori was older than me, out of high school, and she and my mom were pals."

"They just...*left* you?"

More turns. Matt negotiated them. "I was glad they did," he told Phyllis. "I wasn't living with them anymore, hadn't been since I turned sixteen and got a job at the grocery store. I rented a one-bedroom apartment with my first paycheck."

"At sixteen?" Her voice had lost its calm.

The warmth was still there. Matt didn't get it.

"Who'd rent to a sixteen-year-old kid?"

"An old lady who'd taught him in the fourth grade and had a room over her garage."

"Are you still in touch with her?"

He shook his head, slowing as he came to the second bridge. The way was free. He could go. "She died ten years ago."

A happy woman. Her star pupil had still been shining.

It had been another year before he would've killed her with disappointment.

"And in all this time, you've never heard from either your mother or your sister?"

"Not a word." They hadn't actually been on speaking terms. Not after that last big fight when he was sixteen and he'd told them what he thought of them and the life they were living. When he'd denounced everything they stood for, refusing to have anything more to do with them.

He'd not only been incredibly young, he'd been foolish. He'd thought that if he distanced himself from his family, he'd lose the stigma of being related to them. He'd thought he'd stop paying for their choices, their actions.

But he'd been judged by his association with them just the same.

He understood that now. He was a Sheffield and he couldn't escape his past.

But that wasn't going to happen to his child. No child of his was going to be judged by his father's sins. Or made to suffer for them.

If he was certain of nothing else in life, he was certain of that. He'd die before he'd allow another generation to be hurt by the stigma of criminal convictions and jail time. Of coming from losers. And going nowhere because of it.

"Did you have any other family? Aunts, uncles, cousins?"

Oh, yeah. "My dad's younger brother."

"He couldn't take you in?"

"At the time he was serving ten years for auto theft...."

THE RESTAURANT WAS amazing. That was the only word Phyllis could think of—*amazing*. She stared, her eyes darting all over the room. It was a rustic old place, and she could easily believe it had been there for more than a hundred years. A good part of the building hadn't been, Matt had told her, as it had burned in a fire in 1987. But some of the original structure still stood.

There was nothing fancy about the wooden tables and chairs crammed too close together, the cheap tablecloths. Yet it was perfect. They were seated immediately, which Matt said was fortunate since the restaurant didn't take reservations.

At the moment, her stomach was cooperating. She didn't feel even a twinge of the morning sickness that had been causing her such misery over the past few weeks.

"I've never seen so many dollar bills in my life,"

she said for the third time. Since arriving at Tortilla Flat, all their conversation had centered on the restaurant. Every available inch of the inside walls were covered with bills, mostly American one-dollar bills, but other paper currency, as well. Some foreign. Even some checks.

Though she sensed that their conversation—their *real* conversation—was far from over, Phyllis was glad for the respite.

Matt had one hell of a lot of pain bottled up inside him. Phyllis hadn't felt anything that potent in more than a year. Probably not since she'd first met Tory Sanders, struggling with grief for her sister and fear of her ex-husband. She knew that if the situation with Matt was different, if she'd met him at another time, in another way, if she hadn't slept with him, she could probably have helped him.

She would've liked to try. Underneath all the keep-off signs, Matt Sheffield was an intelligent, gentle man. A kind man. At least judging how he'd been with her. And with his students during her symposium.

"People come here from all over the world and leave the money," Matt said after their waiter had taken their drink order, imparted a bit of Tortilla Flat history and left. Matt indicated the newspapers the man had set in front of them.

"The rest of the history is right there, and the article on the second page is the menu."

The place was crowded, with every one of the

fifteen or so tables taken and people milling around in the gift shop just beyond.

"The bills all have names on them," Phyllis said.

"Or business cards tacked to them."

"How many of them do you think there are?"

"I wonder every time I come here, but I have no idea."

"A million maybe?"

"I doubt it. But I know it was a lot more than anyone wanted to lose when the place burned in '87."

"The walls were covered like this back then, too?"

"More so, from what I'm told. I guess the bills were four and five thick in some places."

He looked so comfortable sitting there, sipping from the iced tea the waiter had brought. The perfect host.

Phyllis could hardly believe this was the same man she'd known in Shelter Valley. Or the one she'd driven up with.

He'd shed his jacket, revealing his broad shoulders in the denim shirt he was wearing. It was tucked into another pair of the snug-fitting jeans that had driven Phyllis to insanity that fateful Saturday afternoon.

His black hair and eyes were just as captivating. And those hands, resting so easily on the table…

She guessed it was time they returned to the business at hand. Before she forgot that all it could ever be was business.

"So," she said, leaning forward, hands folded on the table. "Back to medical history. Any allergies in your family?"

"None."

"You aren't allergic to any medications?"

"Not that I know of."

She could do this. Breeze right through without ever really focusing on what was going on. Just get the information and process it later.

"What about blood type?"

"I have one."

Startled, Phyllis brought back her wandering gaze to land on him. He was grinning. The effect was devastating.

Phyllis smiled back. "I assumed so. You wouldn't happen to know what it is, would you?"

"B positive."

She was A positive, which would be just fine.

And then she ran out of questions.

The waiter finally stopped at their table on one of his many trips past. They gave their lunch order. He was having a burger. She'd chosen the taco salad. After that she just sat. And pretended there weren't a million things she wanted to know about him.

She could tell herself that she should ask them in order to safeguard her child's future. But she didn't. She was a psychologist; she knew those tricks.

She was familiar with the various and often complex rationalizations the mind devised, rationalizations that let you do what you wanted when you knew you shouldn't. Focusing on the one reason it was all right to proceed while ignoring the four reasons it wasn't.

Such rationalizations had caught her once—and trapped her.

She wasn't going to be caught again.

Not by the mind's devices. Not by her own devices. And not by being vulnerable to the whims of the male ego.

She'd finally gotten beyond the pain of her divorce. Faced reality. Left useless dreams behind. She'd moved to Shelter Valley and found happiness. She loved the town, her work, helping others. She loved the way people in Shelter Valley made her feel. She finally had a life full of true friends and the things that really mattered.

And she had a baby on the way. She couldn't afford to threaten all of that by doing something foolish—like getting involved with a man who had no place in her new life.

CHAPTER FOUR

MATT HAD NO IDEA how he and Phyllis had ended up sitting on her front step as the afternoon waned. He'd walked her to her door after their trip, she'd asked a question about the presentation he'd helped her with earlier that semester—said she was hoping to have a video made of it for some of her peers who'd attended the symposium. One comment led to another and suddenly, almost an hour later, he became aware of himself sitting there, having a real give-and-take adult conversation for the first time in years.

They still hadn't broached the reason he'd called this meeting. And he wasn't sure how, exactly, he should bring up the subject.

''What about dating?'' he suddenly blurted as her questions about lighting-design techniques finally dwindled.

''No!'' she exclaimed, her shoulders straightening, bringing her breasts into relief against the black velour covering them. ''We already agreed there'll be no involvement between us,'' she added with a little less agitation.

Matt could almost feel the effort it took her to

appear unaffected. So the good doctor had secrets, too.

"I meant *you* dating," he said slowly, wondering just what those secrets might be. "Not us."

"Oh." She paused, her shoulders relaxing as she wrapped her arms around her knees. "Well, not that it's any business of yours, but I don't."

"Don't date?" If he wasn't so detached, he might've been shocked. "Ever?"

"Nope."

"Why the hell not?"

She pierced him with a look he'd have been hard-pressed not to challenge in another life. "This may come as a surprise to you, but not every woman needs a man in her life to be happy." Her eyes dared him to argue with her.

"No, I guess lesbians don't."

"I'm not a lesbian."

"I'm fully aware of that."

She blushed. Looked away.

Matt bit back a grin.

And then quickly sobered as he remembered he wasn't there to enjoy himself.

"It occurred to me yesterday that this…situation we've created makes any relationship you are…or hope to be involved in…difficult. Romantically speaking."

Smooth, Sheffield. Spit that one right out.

"No problem there."

"Oh." Matt nodded, waiting for the relief he was going to be feeling any second. "Good."

What the hell did that mean—*No problem there?* That she was in a relationship—one that had moved beyond dating—and the man was willing to take on Matt's baby? Or that she'd really been speaking of herself and not just hypothetically when she'd said a woman didn't need a man in her life to be happy?

A family, all wearing helmets and gloves with their sweatshirts and jeans, rode by on bikes, two adult-size and two child-size, one with training wheels. Matt and Phyllis watched silently. He wondered if things were as perfect inside that family's house as they appeared on the outside.

"So, you really doing okay?" he asked Phyllis as the family rode slowly around the corner and out of sight.

"I really am."

"You're sure?"

She turned to look at him, her soft green eyes filled with question. "I'm sure," she told him. "Why do you find that so hard to believe?"

Matt shrugged, gazing out at the street. With his forearms resting on his knees, his black leather jacket open, allowing the evening chill to penetrate the thin cotton of his button-down shirt, he contemplated the wisdom of answering her question.

"I guess because I'm having a little trouble with things myself," he finally said.

A quick sideways glance showed him her frown.

Matt focused on the white minivan driving past. A thirty-something short-haired man was driving, a blond woman in the passenger seat. A not-too-tiny hand was plastered to one of the back windows facing them. He'd seen at least one car seat, as well. A family going out to dinner after work?

Or maybe to some kind of ball game? Had that hand in the back belonged to a boy? Was he an aspiring athlete? And if so, did he have any real talent, or were the next few years going to be a real struggle for him?

"What kind of problems are you having?" Phyllis's question, which sounded almost reluctant, reminded Matt that he wasn't sitting there alone. And shouldn't, for the moment, be living vicariously.

"I wouldn't call them problems," he was quick to assure her. Nothing so complicated as a *problem*. "But I'm not an irresponsible man."

"I never thought you were."

He was glad to hear that. Not that it should matter.

"So, the fact that I've fathered a child and am doing absolutely nothing to take responsibility for it isn't going down right with me."

"But I'm not *letting* you do anything."

"I know."

"So the choice is out of your hands."

He pinned her with a hard stare. "Is it?"

Rocking back and forth, her feet leaving the step, then gently touching again, Phyllis nodded. "Of course it is. It's not as if there's anything for you to do. Any role to play. We hardly know each other.''

"I'm the baby's father.''

"He doesn't know that.''

His stomach dropped. "It's a boy?''

"I don't know." She glanced at him and then away. "That was a generic 'he.'''

"Oh.'' Good. For a second there, thinking the baby actually had a sex had made it all seem so much more real. So much more threatening.

He knew that made no sense. Of course the baby had a sex. Whether or not its unprepared parents knew what it was.

"The point is,'' Phyllis said, still hugging her knees, still rocking slightly, "your involvement here is only biological. In the big picture, that doesn't have to mean anything.''

Relief flooded through Matt, almost bringing forth the grin he'd suppressed earlier. Almost, but not quite. A strange, inexplicable sadness got in the way.

"I can't just turn my back on this.''

"You have no choice." She started to rock harder.

"There are always choices." Some much harder to face than others.

"We agreed I'd do this on my own." Her voice had a definite edge to it.

"I know.''

"But you're reneging on that?''

"No." He thought about the past weeks, wondered how he could possibly explain them to her. To himself. Wondered why he even wanted to try.

"So you're going to let me do this alone, but you'd like to be a father to the baby?" She'd lost some of her edge but was still hugging herself tightly. He thought she might be cold, in spite of the thick velour sweater she was wearing.

The air was definitely cooler now that the sun was losing its intensity.

It really wouldn't be good for her to catch a chill.

"I can't be a father."

He hadn't meant the words to come out like that. Wasn't sure he'd meant them to come out at all. Somehow, over the years of observing rather than living, he'd forgotten how to communicate.

"What do you mean, *can't?*" she challenged. "Don't you mean *won't?* That you don't want to?"

No, that wasn't what he'd intended. It had been so long since his wanting had played a part in anything that he no longer even asked himself *what* he wanted.

"You're just going to have to trust me on this one." He bit down hard, controlling the tension gripping him. "I'm not father material! Wouldn't be good for a child."

"That's ridiculous," Phyllis said, apparently not having heard his admonition about trust. Or perhaps it was the fact that he hadn't done anything to earn her trust that had her arguing an inarguable point with him. "You're great with your students," she continued. "Patient, firm. It's obvious they adore you."

No one adored him. No one got that close. He made certain of that. "I control the grade book."

He could feel her eyes on him again. "You really believe that's all it is?"

"Of course." That was all it could be. "I have a past, Phyllis," he told her, sounding a little too adamant. They had to get over this once and for all so they need never visit it again. "I've made mistakes that would inevitably reflect on anyone closely associated with me."

"Everyone reaching our age has made mistakes. Either that or they haven't lived."

"I can't be a father to that child."

He'd grown up the child of a convict. Knew how that fact insidiously wore away at a boy's self-esteem, his confidence. His sense of who he was. Coming from a family of cons did something to a kid, made him something he might not otherwise have been, convinced him of things he didn't even recognize until it was too late.

Matt might not be guilty of the crime of which he was convicted, might even have won his acquittal, but only because the evidence hadn't been strong enough the second time around to pass the "beyond reasonable doubt" provision. No one really knew—except Matt himself—what had happened between him and Shelley Monroe. Shelley wasn't certain herself, although Matt knew full well what she *wanted* to believe, what she chose to believe. She thought Matt had slept with her that day in his office when she'd been too drugged to remember what had happened. It was what she *needed* to think.

He understood that now.

Understood, too, that a lot of what had happened between them was his own damn fault. Shelley had longed for love and acceptance. At fourteen she'd already been conditioned by the life she led, the choices she'd made, to take her validation, her self-worth, from her body. Because of that, she'd needed badly to believe that Matt found her body worthy, that he considered her attractive. And so, like an idiot, he'd given her the verbal praise she'd seemed so desperately to require.

He hadn't even been able to ease his guilt with the knowledge that he'd never ever thought about Shelley as a female. The idea of having sex with a fourteen-year-old girl, no matter how much older than her years, hadn't entered his mind for even a second. But, he had, perhaps, fallen just a little in love with the woman he knew she could someday become.

Which was one of the reasons he sent her a support check every month. He might not be the father of her child, but he wasn't completely free of responsibility for what had happened. Besides, then and now, he saw her potential—a potential she was well on her way to achieving.

Shelley was one of those rare people who had grit

and talent, wit and compassion and that ability to see a bit deeper, go a bit farther, than most people.

Phyllis let out a heavy sigh, bringing Matt back from the hell he'd visited less and less over the past four years—and almost hourly, it seemed, during the past month. She'd stopped rocking. Rested her head on her pulled-up knees.

"What exactly do you want, then?" He could feel her gaze on him, but didn't turn to meet it.

"I'm not sure," he answered honestly. Having come this far, he didn't see that he could answer her in any other way. "I just feel I should be doing *something*. Watching out for you, if nothing else."

She took a quick breath and he held up his hand to forestall the argument he knew was coming. "We hardly know each other," he said, choosing his words carefully. "But at the moment, we share a very intimate problem and I can't seem to forget that.

"Don't get me wrong," he continued when she didn't have anything to say to that. "I'm honestly very glad that you're doing so well with all of this, and I don't want to make things more difficult for you. It just seems as though I'm getting off too easy here. Life doesn't work that way."

"I didn't think of that." Her voice was soft, compassionate, compelling him to meet her gaze. It was as warm as her voice had promised, and though he knew he should, Matt couldn't look away. "What you're saying makes perfect sense," she went on slowly, still reaching inside him with that gentle, open look. "It might seem odd to admit this, considering the circumstances, but I guess I've been the selfish one here."

He had to look away. Or drown. "I'd hardly say that."

"I haven't been fair to you, but I'm not sure how to remedy that."

He wasn't sure, either. And was finding it a little difficult to breathe. "Maybe we should just leave things as they are for the moment," he said, stretching his legs in front of him in preparation for standing.

It was time to go.

"As long as you're really okay..." he added.

"I'm fine," she said, and sounded as if she meant it. She even met his eyes again, but somehow, though their eyes met, her gaze didn't touch him as it had before. "But you—"

"Don't worry about me. I'd say any discomfort I'm feeling is far less than I deserve."

They stood together.

"You'll call me if you need anything?" he asked, looking down at her, reluctant to leave her there— even while he couldn't get away fast enough.

God, she was beautiful.

"I promise," she told him, and he believed her.

And with that he was going to have to be satisfied.

IF PHYLLIS HADN'T LOVED Tory Sanders so much, she'd have skipped her younger friend's baby shower the next day. She'd been nauseated almost every morning that previous week, though thankfully not at all during her time with Matt the day before, but nothing compared to the way she was feeling on Sunday afternoon. The taste of grape juice she'd had during communion at church had turned her stomach, and by two o'clock—the time for Tory's shower—her traitorous insides had not yet righted themselves.

Because the shower was a double one, for Tory and for Randi Foster, both of whom were expecting their first babies within the next six weeks, they'd all decided to have it at Becca Parsons's large home up on the mountain rather than in Phyllis's little bungalow. As she gathered up the presents she'd wrapped the night before, Phyllis couldn't help but be grateful for small blessings.

She'd have died for sure if she'd had to prepare food and tidy her house for the onslaught of all of her friends. As it was, when Cassie came by to pick her up, Phyllis had to make a mad dash from the car and back inside to her bathroom before she was ready to go.

What Cassie didn't know was that the shower was a surprise for her, too. The entire town was turning out to celebrate with their golden girl.

"You have to tell them," Cassie said softly when they were finally under way.

"I know, but not today."

"Why not today?"

Cassie was radiant in her moss-green maternity top and matching slacks. She was wearing her long red hair down these days and looked younger than she had in years. Unlike Phyllis, Cassie was a woman who needed the man she loved beside her.

Thank God he'd decided to end his ten-year absence and return home to the family he'd left behind in Shelter Valley. Phyllis had hated Sam Montford when she'd first heard about him. But after months of getting to know the man, she had to admit she was as fond of him as everyone else in this town.

Cassie was a lucky woman. In so many ways.

"Today is for Tory and Randi," Phyllis answered her friend belatedly. "I don't want to spoil it for them."

"I think a baby shower is a perfect time to tell your friends that you're going to have a baby," Cassie said. Phyllis recognized the tone in her friend's voice. Cassie wasn't planning to give up on this one easily.

And, Phyllis wasn't certain she had the energy to fight her.

"Maybe," she allowed, a partial concession.

"It'd be good to do it with everyone together." Cassie turned onto the road that wound up the mountain to Becca and Will's home—the same road that continued on up to Montford Mansion, the home Cassie's husband would one day inherit.

"Maybe I should wait and tell Will first," Phyllis

said, frowning. "I'm not sure I should drop a bomb like this on my boss in a room full of people."

Will Parsons was the president of Montford University. He'd been the one who'd hired Phyllis away from her Boston College the year before.

"You're afraid he's going to ask too many questions," Cassie said.

She wasn't letting Phyllis get away with anything. "There is that."

"All the better to make the announcement today, then. There'll be so many people talking at once, he won't have a chance to say a word."

"Maybe he won't be there."

"Are you kidding? Randi's his baby sister. He's watching her like a hawk. Besides, other guys are going to be there. Ben. And Zack."

"And Sam," Phyllis said, grinning at her friend. The guys were all coming over after a round of golf. They were going to grill steaks that evening.

Just the thought of it made Phyllis' stomach start to churn again.

"You need me to pull over?" Cassie asked, her quick gaze filled with sympathy as she noticed Phyllis sliding down in her seat, head in her hands.

"Not yet," Phyllis said, trying to concentrate on cool breezes and sheets and showers and anything else that was cool and nonedible. "I don't know what's the matter with me today. It hasn't been nearly as bad as this...until today."

"It happens like that sometimes," Cassie said, a

pregnancy pro now that she was all the way into her sixth month. "The good news is it can go as quickly as it comes."

"Thank God for that."

"So, you still coming over for Thanksgiving?"

"Of course." Phyllis smiled. Hard to believe the holiday was only five days away. "I wouldn't miss it for the world." Cassie, Tory, their families. It was what life was all about.

"I called you a couple of times yesterday," Cassie said as she maneuvered her Taurus slowly up the hill.

"I was gone."

"For hours."

"You checking up on me, Mom?"

"Maybe."

"Matt and I went to Tortilla Flat for lunch."

"Oh?"

"It wasn't like that." Phyllis eyed her black leather boots, deciding they complemented the beige hip-huggers she was wearing with her leopard blouse and black leather vest. She might not be wearing the slacks or top for long, but the boots would still fit in a couple of months, wouldn't they?

"How was it, then?" Cassie asked. If she'd been trying for casual, she failed.

"He just thought we should get together once, share medical information, stuff like that."

"Did he tell you anything about his family? About his life before Shelter Valley?"

"A little."

"And?"

"I don't think he's the cold fish you think he is, Cass," Phyllis said, sitting up. "He had a rough time growing up, and I'm pretty sure there's been some serious stuff since then, but he's a good man. Fair. Conscientious."

Cassie pulled into the Parsons's circular drive, parking the car behind three others already there.

"I'm not telling them today," Phyllis said, looking at the beautiful home that belonged to her very first friends in Shelter Valley. "I'm still early in my term—I need a little more time."

Cassie's expression relaxed as she nodded. "About Matt Sheffield, you're going to be okay, aren't you?" she asked softly.

"You mean I'm not going to do something stupid like fall for him?"

"Okay, maybe."

"Don't worry," Phyllis said, her stomach heaving again. "There's no chance of that at all."

"I'd just hate to see you get hurt."

"I know," Phyllis said, squeezing Cassie's hand. "I don't intend to."

Phyllis knew that not every woman was meant to share her life with a man. She was one of those women. She could handle relationships with men as friends, but that was it.

The ground was too uneven, too treacherous, for a lifetime of one-on-one. Maybe she was too much of a threat. Or perhaps being around her all the time just got old.

Which was fine by her. She'd already tried love and marriage and had no intention of taking those risks again. The one and only time she'd ever come close to losing her grasp on reality had been when she'd been emotionally involved with a man.

Cassie didn't have anything to worry about.

Matt Sheffield couldn't hurt her. Because he wouldn't get the chance.

CHAPTER FIVE

"MR. SHEFFIELD, may I speak with you for a moment?"

Turning from the lighting board, Matt nodded. "Sure, Sophie, what's up? Another problem with Daniel?"

Matt had assigned him to a couple of shows over the semester, in a couple of different capacities. The kid might love the theater, might want to be a techie more than anything else in life, but he just didn't get the technical stuff.

"No."

It was the first week of December. Thanksgiving had came and gone, and they were facing a lull before the end-of-semester holiday shows. The only shows they had right now were a couple of concerts at the end of the week—the jazz band and a choral concert. While neither of those took more than basic lighting, the sound requirements would pose a challenge.

"Then what?" Matt asked. It was warm in the theater, yet Sophie was all bundled up in a turtleneck shirt with a bulky sweater over top.

"I'm just trying to figure out what I should do

next semester,'' she said. She seemed even more distracted than she'd been over the past month, almost as though she was having trouble concentrating.

"I'd think that must be pretty clear at this point," Matt said, studying her. He wasn't going to get involved. He wasn't. But damn, the girl didn't look good. Her face was far too drawn. He wondered if, under those bulky clothes, the rest of her was as skinny. "You've only got another three semesters before you graduate, and you know what courses you need."

"I know." She nodded, sinking down on the couch along the wall. The same one Matt had shared with Phyllis Langford.

Phyllis. A day hadn't gone by that he hadn't thought of her. The mother of his child.

He should be doing something. But there was nothing he could do—*nothing* was the one thing Phyllis had asked of him. He was equally responsible for her predicament, though, and she was carrying all the load. And not just physically.

Hitting the appropriate keys to save the work he'd been doing, Matt waited for Sophie to say whatever she'd come to say.

"I'm thinking about quitting school."

He stopped, turned slowly to face her, leaning back against the worktable as he carefully measured his response.

"Why?"

She shrugged. "I don't know."

Matt bit back a word he shouldn't say in front of a student. "If you have no good reason to quit, then why not stay in school?" he asked, instead.

"I'm just so confused."

"Have you talked to anyone about it?" *Get her to a counselor,* his mind was screaming. It was what he should've done with Shelley all those years ago. Law officials had told him so. His lawyer had told him so. The school principal had told him—

"I'm talking to *you,*" she said.

Her eyes were huge when she looked up at him. Matt's stomach tensed. He couldn't do this. *Didn't* do this.

"I teach lighting design," he muttered.

"You're the only person who's given a damn about me in the two years I've been at Montford."

"It may seem that way," he said slowly, panic shooting through him as he quickly relived the past two and a half years with his star pupil. Had he ever, unwittingly, done anything to give her any indication that he regarded her as more than a student? "But I'm sure that there are other people here who care about you."

"You make me believe I'm worth something."

The tears pooling in her eyes spoke more to him than her words. "You *are* worth something," he said before he could analyze the significance of his remark. Lighting design and theater operation were what he spoke to his students about. It was all about art. Craft.

Never about life.

Not anymore.

"My mom's getting divorced again."

Matt waited. Home lives were off-limits. Because he couldn't trust himself to know when enough was enough, Matt adhered very strictly to the promise he'd made himself when Will Parsons had given him this chance at Montford. He'd teach. He'd give his students every bit of knowledge he could give them about his area of expertise. And nothing else.

There were school counselors and trained professionals to help students with their personal problems.

"It's the fifth time."

Matt knew that. He'd heard Sophie—and many of his other regular students—speak about their lives during the long hours they all spent together getting ready for a show. During a show week they were often at the theater until midnight. Even later for breakdowns. He heard. He didn't comment.

He gathered together the specs he'd been working on, put them in a folder.

"She's a slut."

His mother had been one of those, too. Cringing, Matt leaned against the lighting board again, a frown on his face.

"What does this have to do with your staying in school?" It wasn't the question he wanted to ask, the words he wanted to say. They were just the only ones he was *allowed* to say.

"What's the point?"

"To make something of yourself," Matt answered immediately. "You have great talent, Sophie, a natural feel. It's not just technical work to you, it's art. You know how to help people get more out of their productions. With enough training, you'll go far in this business."

Shoulders slumped, she didn't even seem to hear him. Not judging by the sullen look on her face.

Something had happened to this girl.

And it wasn't any of his damn business. She was just a student. Someone who would pass in and out of his life—someone who'd be there long enough to get lighting design information from him. And nothing else.

"You look like you've lost some weight," he said. *Get her to a counselor.*

She shrugged, her long blond hair as dull as the expression in her eyes.

"You been eating okay?" Too personal. He shouldn't have asked.

"Yeah."

Nodding, Matt picked up some sample gels he'd been perusing earlier. Sophie handed him the envelope they'd come in. She'd broken a nail, her right index finger, and done nothing to fix it. That was odd, too. One of Sophie's trademarks was her long, always wildly polished fingernails.

"Sign up for classes for next semester," he said suddenly. He had to get her out of the theater before he did something stupid. Like try to help her figure out whatever was bothering her.

Her gaze was confused as she looked up at him. Confused and helpless. "You really think I should?"

"I think it would be ludicrous not to." Was she doubting her abilities because of the mistakes she'd made that semester? Did she think that being distracted now and then negated her natural talent?

"But what kind of girl goes for a career as a theater technician?"

Or was there a boyfriend involved in her sudden doubts?

"Lots of girls do," he said with confidence. This was a question that was perfectly in order for him to answer. "Smart girls. Artistic girls. Girls who love the theater as much as you do."

"You don't think it makes me seem too masculine?"

Matt wanted to pull up a chair and sit down. He stood awkwardly by the door, instead. "No."

He might have told her how utterly ridiculous she was being. That she was a classically beautiful college co-ed. And that she was far too smart to wear any labels imposed on her by people who didn't know any better. But he couldn't.

Not his place. *Get her to a counselor.*

She stood up, watching him for a moment, and Matt had no idea what was going on behind those troubled blue eyes. "Okay, I'll go register."

And then she was gone.

Though he'd seemingly won that round, Matt stared after her, uneasy. He didn't know what had just happened. What the entire conversation had really been about. But he had the distinct impression it wasn't good.

NOT FEELING ANY BETTER that afternoon, Matt tried to concentrate on the schedule in front of him. He needed five crew members for next week's Winter Dance concert. And that many plus more for the two-week Theater Department production of Charles Dickens's *A Christmas Carol* following that. And they'd just had a request from the Phoenix Symphony for extra rehearsal time for the show they were doing in Shelter Valley the week before Christmas.

He volunteered himself for that show. He could work as many hours as needed during the Christmas holiday. It wasn't as if he had any shopping to do—or anyone to celebrate with.

That thought brought him a measure of relief.

Until he wondered what Phyllis Langford was doing for Christmas. Did she have family to go home to? Family she'd have to break her news to? Or had she already told them all?

He wondered how her loved ones had reacted—or would react—to the news.

Or if she even had any loved ones. Seemed like something he should know about her. But he couldn't figure out why he felt that way. It had nothing to do with him.

The phone on his desk rang, and Matt grabbed it, glad for the reprieve. "Sheffield," he said more brusquely than necessary.

"Matt?"

"Phyllis?" How could he immediately know her voice when he'd only talked to her on the phone a time or two?

"You busy?"

He glanced at the schedule. And then at the stacks of paper on his desk, all concerning new projects, all waiting for something or other from him. He could be there till midnight.

But at least he'd taught his last class for the day.

"Not at the moment. What's up?" He hadn't seen or heard from her since their trip to Tortilla Flat two weeks before.

"I really hate to do this," she started, and then stopped. Her unusually hesitant tone had him instantly alert.

"Do what?"

"Ask you to drive me to Phoenix."

Matt dropped the pencil he'd been holding. "Something wrong?"

"I don't think so," she said quickly, her words more confident than her tone. "I'm just...bleeding a little."

"Did you call your doctor?"

"Yes. She doesn't think it's anything, but she

wants to see me. She did say, though, that I probably shouldn't be driving all that way by myself.''

"Of course you shouldn't." Matt reached for the keys he'd thrown onto the corner of his desk when he'd come in that morning. "Where are you?"

"In my office."

"Here on campus?"

"Yeah. Psych 132. I'm really sorry about this—" Matt cut her off. "Don't be ridiculous."

"Cassie's in surgery, Randi had an away basket-ball game and I can't get hold of Becca or Tory. I could call Martha Moore or even Will, but to be honest with you, I haven't told anyone except Cassie about my pregnancy yet—"

"I'm on my way over," Matt said. She didn't need to make excuses to him. He was responsible for her current situation. It was right that she call him.

As Matt checked out with his secretary, locked his office and hurried across campus, he couldn't help offering up a small prayer that the baby would be okay.

He'd been plagued over the past few weeks by the need to take some kind of responsibility. This wasn't quite what he'd had in mind.

THE BLEEDING WAS nothing to worry about. It had stopped by the time Phyllis and Matt reached Phoenix.

When her lab work came back, she was hospitalized overnight, anyway. She'd been throwing up so much she was dehydrated. As someone who wasn't exactly uninformed about medical matters, Phyllis felt stupid for not seeing the signs or taking more precautions.

Embarrassed, lying in the bed with the IV drip hanging beside her, she wished she could slide under the covers when Matt knocked on her open door.

"You decent?"

If you called wearing a gown that had no back to it decent. "Yeah." She pulled the covers up under her chin.

"Dr. Mac says you'll only need to be here overnight. Luckily they caught things before they could get too serious."

She nodded, feeling at a complete disadvantage as he sat, fully clothed, in the chair beside her bed.

"Why didn't you tell me you'd been having such a problem with morning sickness?"

Raising her bed with the fingertip control, Phyllis said, "Why would I? It's a normal part of pregnancy."

"It must've been pretty severe to require an IV drip."

Phyllis couldn't argue with him there. "I'm really sorry about this. You can head on back home. I'll call Cassie tonight and she'll make sure someone's here in the morning to pick me up."

"I've got nobody waiting for me at home," he

said, his hands steepled under his chin as he gazed at her.

For one crazy moment, Phyllis remembered how those hands had felt on her body....

"I figured I might as well keep you company tonight."

She swallowed. "That's not necessary."

"Might be good for us to talk a little more," he said, almost as though she hadn't said a word. If it wasn't for his slight frown, Phyllis would've thought he hadn't heard her at all.

"It occurred to me that I don't even know if you have any living family."

She didn't understand why that should matter to him. She'd repeatedly told him her pregnancy wasn't his responsibility.

Phyllis wasn't planning to get to know him any better than she already did.

He wasn't father material. He'd said so himself.

"My parents are both gone," she said. She'd *meant* to tell him to leave. "My father was fifty, my mom in her forties when they had me. I was an only child."

He nodded, still watching her.

"You really don't have to stay."

"It's the least I can do," he said, his tone of voice warning her she wasn't going to win this one. "I'll get a room in the motel across the street and be back here in the morning. You said your first class doesn't start till eleven. We should be able to make it home in plenty of time for you to shower and get to school.''

The doctor had said that if everything continued to look good, there was no reason Phyllis couldn't be released after her eight-o'clock rounds.

She'd also said Phyllis should be getting more rest. That the bleeding was nothing serious at the moment, but these things were frequently warnings of future problems. She'd warned Phyllis to slow down. She could work, take care of business, but she wasn't to do any heavy lifting or anything that required exertion.

She'd also said Phyllis was already starting to show and seemed a bit surprised by that.

And she'd said all of it when Matt was standing right there, listening.

''You really shouldn't have told Dr. Mac that you're the baby's father,'' Phyllis said now, frowning as she thought of the unexpected repercussions she was facing from the day's phone call. She'd expected an impersonal ride into the city and an equally detached ride home. A bit of small talk maybe, but that was it. Then she would've thanked him and said goodbye.

''I had to. Otherwise, they weren't going to tell me what was happening.''

''I didn't intend to name you on the birth certificate.''

His eyelids lowered. If she hadn't been trained to notice such things, Phyllis would have missed the hurt he'd quickly concealed. And the relief that immediately followed.

"You still don't have to," he said.

"Dr. Mac—"

"Knows only what I told her. How you fill out your child's birth certificate is entirely up to you."

He was right, of course, but—

"You never seem to take that ring off," Matt said, gesturing toward her fingers that were busily twisting the opal ring on her right hand. "Does it have some significance?"

"It was my mother's."

Silence fell. And lingered for several seconds.

"Sounds like you're going to need a little help around the house during the next few months," he finally said.

"I can manage," Phyllis assured him, adding, "I've got enough friends to build a house, let alone keep one up."

The prospect of further involvement was untenable. In the first place because she knew he didn't want to be there.

And in the second...

"How many leather jackets do you have?" She'd seen two so far, and he looked damned good in them.

"Three."

"Black, brown and...?"

"Maroon."

Trying to ignore the interest his dark eyes were

stirring inside her, Phyllis looked at the tube attached to her arm.

"You feeling okay?" he asked.

He was attentive, she had to give him that. Far more attentive than a man in his position should be. Especially when she had to remain completely immune to him, for a lot of reasons.

An almost impossible feat after she'd slept with him, Phyllis was beginning to discover.

Which was why he had to stay the hell away from her.

"I'll come over once a week and do any heavy chores that need doing."

"What?" Where had that come from?

"I'm partially responsible for this situation," Matt said, leaning forward, his elbows on his knees. "There's no reason for your friends to be put out when I'm perfectly capable of doing whatever needs to be done until you're up and going again."

There *was* a good reason. Phyllis didn't think it was a smart idea to have him around.

"Please."

And then she saw that look in his eyes. The one she'd seen when they went to Tortilla Flat. The one that had been haunting her ever since. Matt Sheffield was a man carrying around some pretty deep hurts.

And Phyllis, a healer of hurts, couldn't refuse the father of her baby this little bit of peace he was seeking. If he'd feel better about himself by helping her out, then she could certainly put up with seeing him occasionally.

He wanted a relationship between them even less than she did, if that was possible. She'd laid down her rules and he'd readily agreed to abide by them. The baby was all hers.

In the past weeks he'd been as good as his word and had left her alone.

She was in control. She felt sure of what she wanted. What she didn't want. Knowledge was freedom.

As long as she knew which turns to avoid, she'd be fine.

And she knew. She'd spent long years learning every last one of them.

CHAPTER SIX

GOD, SHE WAS LOVELY. Her short, sassy red hair splayed on the pillow propped behind her head, Phyllis made a face at him while a nurse checked her blood pressure.

Matt grinned, more relaxed then he'd been in... forever. This woman was easy to talk to.

His kid was going to be one lucky son of a gun growing up with her for a mother.

"Perfectly normal," the nurse said to the accompaniment of ripping Velcro. Once the cuff was removed, the woman made a note on the piece of paper she was holding and left the room with a swish-swish of panty hose and rubber-soled shoes.

"Guess the personality gods skipped her," Phyllis said as soon as the nurse had closed the door to the private room.

"She was just lusting after your French fries." Opting to forgo hospital food, Matt had made a run at dinnertime, returning with burgers and fries for him and Phyllis to share.

"She could've had them. I'm stuffed."

"And you haven't gotten sick once since we've been here."

Phyllis grimaced. "It usually happens in the morning."

As the hours had passed that afternoon—surprising Matt with their swiftness—he'd found himself having an increasingly hard time keeping his eyes from straying to her breasts, hidden and yet revealed by the thin cotton of the hospital shift she was wearing. He might not know the woman well, but he sure remembered the feel of those breasts....

"You really don't have to stay," Phyllis said for about the fiftieth time, laying her arm gingerly on the mattress beside her.

Her hand looked so slender, so fragile, with the IV needle inserted and taped to the top of it. She was going to have a bruise there in the morning.

He'd gladly have borne it for her.

"I've got nothing else to do," he told her now. "But if you want to sleep or watch TV or something, go right ahead."

"I don't watch a lot of television."

He didn't, either. "Do you like to read?"

They'd already covered favorite foods, recent and not-so-recent movies and music that afternoon. Phyllis was a fascinating combination of classic and fad.

"I love to read," she said now, one hand resting her cup of takeout coffee on the hospital sheet covering her lap. "I read at least a chapter of something everyday. How about you?"

Matt nodded. Reading was his salvation. His closest friends lived between the well-worn pages of the books lying all around his house. "I'm reading a great nonfiction book right now. *Our Sacred Honor.* Ever heard of it?"

She shook her head. Her attention seemed to be fully engaged while she waited for him to continue.

It had been so long since Matt had done this—just sat with another adult and experienced a normal human interaction, one not related to his work—that the impact of her attentiveness came as something of a shock.

But not a threat. This was a moment out of time for both of them. Life was suspended for these hours, and they understood that. Understood each other.

"It's by William Bennett, not anyone I've ever read before." Guard down, Matt warmed to his subject. "It's about the flaws and foibles of the people we consider our heroes. Our cultural icons." He paused. "Did you know that George Washington had a violent temper? One he worked very diligently to control?"

"I'd never heard that before."

"Thomas Jefferson died more than one-hundred-thousand dollars in debt."

"No way!"

"Yep." Matt nodded.

"That was a lot of money in those days."

It was a lot of money today, too. More than four times the amount Matt sent off each year, making what reparation he could.

"I do know Abraham Lincoln was prone to depression," Phyllis said.

"Some say he was bipolar, but he certainly didn't let it slow him down. He, too, struggled to control his temperament so it didn't interfere with the job he was here to do."

Phyllis widened her eyes. "He was a man of almost unbelievable strength and self-reliance."

Matt nodded. "Ben Franklin had a thing for 'lowly women,' as he called them."

"Prostitutes?"

Matt shrugged carelessly. "Don't know if he paid them, but immoral women, at least."

"Wasn't he married?"

"Yep." But Matt knew firsthand that a little thing like marriage didn't stop a man from taking what he wanted. Or a woman, either, for that matter.

"It's fascinating, don't you think?"

"Yeah. I wonder how much flack Bennett's taken for writing this stuff."

"I hope none," Phyllis said, raising her knees beneath the covers, reminding Matt what she was—and wasn't—wearing under them.

It was kind of hard to be with her in a bedroom, even if the room was in a hospital, without remembering that they'd had some pretty incredible sex together.

"Why do you say that?" he asked, forcing himself to concentrate on the topic at hand—to return to the innocuous place they were occupying for the evening.

"Because he's done us all a huge favor," she said, her eyes alight as she spoke with a fervor that Matt admired even while he wondered where on earth she was going with this. "Think about it," she continued. "We've had these men held up to us all our lives. From the time we're in grade school, we hear about their greatness. We're raised to believe that we, too, can make a difference, that if we could be like these men, even a little, our lives would have merit."

Matt frowned. "And you think it's great that because of Bennett we're now disillusioned?"

"No! I'm not disillusioned, are you?"

Matt didn't have any illusions left to lose. Hadn't since he was about two.

"Don't you see?" Phyllis said, sitting forward to place her cup on the bedside table.

Matt got a glimpse of her almost-bare back and looked quickly away.

"These men *were* great. They accomplished miraculous things. And they were human, too. Knowing that doesn't take away their greatness. It makes it *more* impressive—and potentially obtainable for the rest of us imperfect human beings lumbering around on this earth."

He thought about that. "I like the way you think."

She looked startled for a second, and then lowered her eyes. An unexpected reaction from a woman who wore her confidence as easily as she wore her stylish clothes.

"I had a student stop by to see me today." His words slid out into the safe environment they'd built in this room.

"And?"

Needless to say, they both had students coming to see them. It was the nature of their business. So she'd know there was more to his observation.

"Her name is Sophie. She's been in the theater program for the past couple of years, and I've had a lot of opportunity to work with her. She's the best damn techie I've ever had."

"Kind of an unusual profession for a girl, isn't it? Don't they have to do a lot of heavy lifting, what with sets and all? And what about pulling those curtains up and down?"

Slouching in the high-backed armchair, Matt lifted his feet to the rail on the side of her bed. "Maybe it used to be, but it's not so unusual to see girls working behind the scenes today. Sophie's more than just a good technical crew member, though. She's an artist. Bring a show into the theater, and by the time she's done with lights and scrims and sound, it has a whole new depth. Professionalism."

"So what's the problem?" Phyllis was frowning as she waited for his reply.

"I'm not sure." He shook his head, not even sure why he'd brought up the subject. It wasn't as if there was anything he could do to help the girl. Other than encourage her to stay in school. Which he'd already done.

Send her to a counselor. The words were never far from the surface of his mind when a student's personal problems entered a work situation.

It suddenly dawned on Matt that he was looking at a counselor. Maybe not one whose job description currently included therapy sessions, but one who'd certainly been trained in the field.

"Sophie's been…acting strange all semester." He spoke slowly, weighing his words. Keeping the necessary distance. "She missed a couple of cues the last time she called a show, she's been late, missed some classes, been impatient with her fellow crew members."

She'd lost weight, seemed distracted, was dressing differently—more sloppily, always wearing bulky clothes. But those things all crossed the line that Matt was not going to cross again. The line between schoolwork and personal life.

Phyllis nodded, seeming to gather information from Matt's eyes, as well as from the words he was saying. "Could it be boyfriend trouble?"

"I wouldn't know."

"You don't know if she's recently broken up with anyone?"

The same guy had been hanging around since the previous spring. He was still hanging around.

Matt shook his head, shrugging. "I don't discuss my students' private lives with them."

"Maybe not in any detail, but some conversation is only natural. Especially considering how much out-of-classroom time you spend with these kids. From the little I've seen, you guys practically live together during show weeks."

"Their private lives are none of my business."

"Of course they're your business, Matt," Phyllis said, tilting her head as she studied him. "You're a teacher, just like I am. Helping kids is what we do. You can't do your job and not know things about them."

"Maybe in your field."

"In any field."

Not in his.

"It's probably just boyfriend trouble," Phyllis said, reverting to her original suggestion with no further argument. Matt would have left if she hadn't backed off.

"Probably," he murmured, although he didn't really think so.

"I'd keep an eye on her," she added, looking thoughtful. "A star student missing classes could be indicative of trouble somewhere."

"Keep an eye on her?" Matt asked.

"I've seen you with your students, Matt. You're good with them. Value them."

He did? He taught lighting design. The art of putting on shows.

"You encourage them, trust them by assigning

tasks and then not standing over them every step of the way. You go along with their solutions.''

"Not always.''

"It wouldn't mean anything if you approved of *everything* they did. You're also teaching them about standards. You're showing them that you trust them to meet your expectations.''

He just taught. Nothing else.

"Your trust in them also builds self-confidence. And in turn, teaches them to trust you.''

Matt wasn't sure that was a responsibility he could accept. He knew he was never going to overstep his teacher-student boundaries again, but all it would take was getting just a little too friendly. Something could easily be misunderstood or blown out of proportion, and it would all come out. The past. Shelley.

And he would be crucified.

He knew how these things worked.

"Obviously this Sophie feels she can trust you. Which is why she came to you today.''

"I teach lighting design.''

"I'm just suggesting you keep an eye on things, Matt, not counsel her.''

He nodded. Yeah, he knew those ropes.

"If I notice anything more, I'll send her to counseling,'' he said.

He left shortly after that, hoping Phyllis would be able to get a good night's sleep. He didn't expect to sleep much himself. Not while he was feeling responsible for the fact that this woman was lying in the hospital with an IV stuck in her hand because he hadn't been more careful about protecting her all those weeks ago.

And not after their last conversation, either. It was always there. The past. Haunting him. Waiting to rear its ugly head.

Yet, as he let himself into his room in the motel across from the hospital, stripped down to his briefs and slid between the sheets, Matt felt strangely relaxed. Phyllis Langford was easy to talk to. Even for a man as out of practice with friendly conversation as he was.

She thought he was a good teacher....

He fell asleep almost as soon as his head hit the pillow.

MATT STOPPED BY Phyllis's house the next night after work. She saw him pull up in front of her bungalow, watched him get out of his truck, lock the door. Her first impulse was to deny him access to her house—and to her life. After last night, the hours they'd spent talking, his tending to her without complaint, she liked him even more than she had that day she'd been so desperate to sleep with him.

Liking a man was a step she couldn't take. One step invariably led to the next....

And then, as she watched him make his way slowly up her walk, hands in the pockets of his jeans, head bent, she remembered that she was going to help him find a measure of peace. Matt Sheffield was a good man. She could feel his goodness every time she was with him.

He was also a man with secrets. Secrets that might be hidden but certainly weren't forgotten. At least not by him. She could feel that, too.

Maybe because he was the father of her unborn baby, which gave her some kind of physical connection to him, or maybe because she was who she was and sometimes saw things in people that others couldn't, Phyllis refused to keep turning her back on him.

Protect herself she would. Of course. Always. But she had a strong feeling she could help this man— and that was something she could no longer ignore.

Her inability to mind her own business, as her ex-husband put it was part of the problem with her and romantic relationships. Most men didn't like to be probed, didn't like their pain exposed to others, examined. Phyllis was a natural prober.

Sometimes people were suffering agonies that could be eased. Sometimes healing came from viewing the source of pain in a different light. Or learning to release the past. The world was too filled with hurts that *couldn't* be fixed to let stand those that could.

Matt Sheffield was a man who needed healing.

She waited until he knocked on the door before going to open it.

"Matt, hi," she said, pulling it wide.

He was wearing the black leather jacket. And—

once again—looked far too good. He stepped into her tiny foyer. "I thought I'd get a start on whatever needs doing," he said, glancing around at the side table still holding the mail she'd brought in, the archway into her living room, the coatrack by the door, the picture of King's Chapel in Boston that hung on the opposite wall.

"I just got home this morning," she reminded him, closing the door. It was okay to have him here. To shut them in together. Because this was for him. "I haven't had much time to get behind on things."

"But you weren't planning to be laid up. There might be stuff you'd been planning to do that you can't do now."

His hands were still in his pockets, but his gaze was direct as it met hers. He was glad to see her.

She was strangely glad to see him, too.

"I'm not really clear on what I can't do," she told him. Her eyes remained on his.

"Taking out the trash, for starters," he said. He was almost smiling as he watched her. While Phyllis was generally aware of nuances that other people missed, she suspected she wasn't the only one hearing the unspoken conversation between them.

"No heavy lifting, Dr. Mac said," Phyllis reminded him. "Trash isn't heavy."

"And carrying laundry baskets."

"My laundry isn't heavy, either." She refused to be the first to look away. His black eyes were almost daring her.

"Could be you have a leaky faucet."

"My wrench isn't heavy."

"Maybe you need some groceries."

Okay, carrying bags of groceries probably wasn't a good idea, but... "I don't. Just went shopping on the weekend."

The tiniest hint of a grin lifted one corner of his mouth.

"How long has it been since you gassed up and washed your car?"

Though she really tried not to, Phyllis gave him a full-fledged grin. "Saturday."

"What about preparing a nursery?"

She blinked. And turned her head. She hadn't let herself think about that yet. There were too many other things to deal with first. Like prenatal care. Maternity clothes. Diet. Vitamins.

College funds.

It was an awful lot for one person to handle all alone. And the way to manage overwhelming tasks was to break them up into manageable portions.

Matt headed down the hall, past the living room and toward the back of the house. "I'm assuming you're going to need some furniture moved."

Yes, but... "Not tonight," Phyllis said, hoping none of the panic she was fighting was evident in her voice.

He glanced at her over his shoulder. "I didn't mean tonight. I just thought we might take a look and come up with some ideas."

He was so damn sweet. How could she say no?

She followed him down the hall and when he was turning toward her bedroom, said, "It's over here," and guided him to the room Tory Sanders had used during her months staying here.

The room Phyllis had lovingly prepared for her best friend, Tory's older sister, Christine.

"You use this only as a guest room?" Matt asked, taking in the twin beds, the dresser, the closet doors across the room.

"Now I do," Phyllis said. "It used to be an office, but I turned it into a bedroom when a friend of mine came to stay."

He looked over at her and then back at the room. "She stay long?"

"*She* didn't stay at all." Maybe because she felt as though she knew him after their time together the day before, Phyllis found herself being open about something she normally wouldn't have shared with him.

"Do you know Tory Sanders?"

"The woman who taught English last fall, posing as her dead sister?"

"Yeah. Her sister, Christine, was my best friend. She was on her way out here from Boston, where we're all from, bringing Tory with her. She was killed in a car accident in New Mexico."

His eyes narrowed. And softened. "I'm sorry."

Phyllis blinked away her tears. "Me, too."

"What happened?"

Tired suddenly, Phyllis sat down on the twin bed that had remained empty all those months Tory had been with her. Christine's bed.

"You want the official story or the real one?"

He took a seat on the corner of the opposite bed, his hands resting on his thighs. "The real one."

"Tory was divorced, on the run from an abusive ex-husband, whose daddy had been buying his way out of trouble his entire life," Phyllis related, going back to those months in Boston when she'd ached right along with Christine as they waited for word from Tory. "Her ex was rich, spoiled, used to getting whatever he wanted. And he wanted Tory. She'd escape, hide in some small town or other, but he'd always find her. And he'd punish her for going every time."

Matt's lips thinned. "Even after they were divorced?"

"Especially after they were divorced. He was more desperate then."

Matt nodded.

"He also made it very clear that he'd rather see her dead than with another man. He'd always been insanely jealous. He'd even forbidden her from entering college because he didn't trust her around all the young jocks."

"He was older than she was?"

"Quite a bit. Tory was barely out of high school when she married him."

"And her parents approved?"

"Her mother was dead. And her stepfather—that's a whole other story. Suffice it to say, the stepfather died serving a life sentence."

"The world's filled with bastards like that."

"Or at least the prisons are. Anyway, Christine got the teaching job out here so she could get Tory away from Bruce. It didn't work. He caught up with them in New Mexico, ran their car off the road, killing Christine and injuring Tory pretty badly, too."

"They got him, I hope?"

Phyllis sneered. "Yeah, right. The ruling was accidental death. One car. No one at fault."

Matt sat forward, his gaze intent. "So he's still out there, looking for Tory?"

"No." Phyllis shook her head. "The hospital officials thought Tory was the sister who'd been killed. Bruce was smart enough to stay away from the crime scene himself, but he sent some guys to verify the pronouncement. He had Tory trailed for months, but when he was finally satisfied that she really was Christine, he killed himself. Despite all the agony he put her through, he couldn't face living without her."

"God, what a mess."

"Yeah." Some people just weren't made for romantic love, Phyllis knew. Couldn't handle the negative emotions that came along with the bliss. Bruce, Tory's husband, had been one of those people.

Phyllis was another.

"You miss her a lot."

"Yeah."

"I'm sorry."

Meeting his eyes, seeing the very real emotion there, Phyllis started to cry. "Thanks," she said, letting the tears roll slowly down her cheeks while she continued to hold his gaze.

He didn't move, didn't touch her. But Phyllis felt as though he'd wrapped his arms around her, holding her tightly. He'd lent her his strength.

Making everything just a little easier.

CHAPTER SEVEN

SOPHIE CURTIS'S ALARM woke her up from a nice dream about her parents. Reaching over to shut it off so she could get back to sleep, she cursed when her knuckles hit her desk chair, instead. *Oh yeah.* She was in the dorm. Not at home where she would've been if her father hadn't decided to take off with his secretary all those years ago and leave her mom behind to fall apart—and to marry every man who was halfway decent to her.

Damn.

She rolled over, feeling groggy and disoriented. She knew her dizziness came from hunger, and she kind of liked that sensation. In the first place, it slowed down the thinking process a little bit—always a relief to Sophie, whose mind never gave her a moment's peace. And it also meant she was strong, in control. She hadn't pigged out—eaten too much—yesterday.

Peeking out through the lashes of one eye, Sophie determined that her roommate had made it to her first class. Good. She didn't feel like being chatty this morning.

What she felt like doing was going back to sleep.

And maybe she would. She could sleep through breakfast. And lunch, too.

But she had her advanced lighting-design class today. An entire hour with Matt. And if she was lucky and he had them work on their individual projects, she'd probably have some time alone with him.

Out of bed, Sophie stumbled to the bathroom. Then she headed, naked, to stand sideways in front of the floor-length mirror on her closet door. Damn. She ran her hand down her belly. There was still a slight bulge.

With a heavy heart, she pulled out the scale she had shoved in the back of her closet and stepped on to it. A hundred and one. Down another pound.

Feeling a little better, she looked in the mirror again. The bulge was still there. She wondered if maybe something was wrong with her.

She shook her head. No. She was just scaring herself. Most people had a bit of a rounded shape to them. Except models who, everyone knew, were anorexic and unhealthy.

So what was she going to wear this morning? Something tight to reveal her legs and butt so Matt could see how much weight she'd lost. But a bulky top. She couldn't have him seeing that bulge.

He'd told her once that blue was her color. Because of her eyes. She pulled a blue angora sweater out of her bottom drawer.

Okay, so he'd been speaking of a series of lights she'd put together. He'd mentioned that they were the blue that was about the color of her eyes. And that she tended to use blues a lot, probably because they complemented her, and students tended to lean toward the colors they felt good about.

But she'd known what he meant. He liked her in blue.

Pulling on the black jeans she'd saved to wear for him today, Sophie frowned until she could fasten the button at the top and see that the waistband was a little loose.

If she ever got her chance with Matt, which she was sure she would one of these days, she wanted to be absolutely sure she was perfect for him.

More perfect than she'd been for Jason. And Stu. And Paul. She'd been good in bed—it was the one thing she knew she could do well—but not good enough to hold on to any of them. Oh, Paul still hung around, just like he'd been hanging around for more than a year, but she knew he'd taken that cheerleader to bed.

Just like her father and his secretary.

No, what Sophie needed was a real man like Matt Sheffield. He'd know the value of a beautiful woman's body. He'd never just use her for momentary satisfaction. He was strong and true.

Look how nice he'd been to her when she'd finally gotten up the courage to seek him out the other day. She'd been on the verge of tears, ready to give up on everything, and just being with him had made her feel better. She'd felt resolute and focused, able to cope again.

And he'd practically begged her to stay in his classes.

God. She loved him so much it hurt.

PHYLLIS STARTED BLEEDING again the next afternoon. Heart pounding, she stood there in her bathroom, looking at the evidence. It was only a little bit, she told herself. Not enough to be significant.

But it could get worse.

She could lose her baby.

She couldn't bear the thought.

With shaking hands she carefully changed her underwear, then pulled on the jeans she'd been changing into after work. She reached for the soap she kept under her sink for hand-washables. Generally she used it for her panty hose.

When she'd first found out she was pregnant, she hadn't thought it was good news. She was single. With no plans of ever not being that way. She was a college professor, had to conform to a certain moral code. Her life was mapped out just the way she wanted it. And the map didn't include a baby.

And yet...the baby had become real to her. Real and precious. And her map had been redrawn.

After a quick call to her doctor's office, Phyllis had a stern talk with herself, which only partially worked. The doctor had asked a couple of questions and then assured Phyllis she had nothing to worry about. She was to take it easy, watch out for symptoms, but Dr. Mac thought the day's spotting was just residual from earlier in the week.

She'd examined Phyllis after the initial incident and found everything exactly as it should be. Some women had a bit of spotting in the early months of pregnancy, she'd explained. When it was as little as Phyllis was experiencing, it was usually no big deal. Before she hung up, she told Phyllis the signs to watch for, just in case.

Usually no big deal. Not *always* no big deal. Which meant that at some time or other, for some woman or other, it *was* a big deal. And what if she started seeing the signs Dr. Mac had described? What if the bleeding got worse?

Stop it. She was letting her mind run away with her. Being ridiculous. She knew better than this. She needed to distract herself, think about something else until the panic subsided and she was her rational self again.

Matt. She had to call Matt.

Portable phone to her ear, it dawned on her that, although she'd only phoned him once before, she knew his number by heart. He might be on her list of support people at the moment—the bottom of her list—but she didn't need to know his number. She'd have to put it out of her mind. Forget it.

There was really no reason to call him. Nothing was wrong. And she had no heavy lifting to be done.

This baby was her responsibility. Not his.

She might as well hang up.

"Sheffield."

He was still in his office. She had the feeling he spent a lot of time there.

"I, uh, I'm sorry. I shouldn't have called."

"Phyllis? Something wrong?" His voice had sharpened.

"No." She felt like an idiot. "I really am sorry. I was about to hang up when you answered."

"Why?"

"Because I was just being weak and stupid for a moment there, but I'm fine now. It was totally unlike me and won't happen again. I can't believe I did it. I don't even want to talk to you. Put it down to hormones and forget it ever happened. See ya." The words flew out in a rush, and when she finished that last sentence and was afraid of what else might come out, Phyllis pushed the Off button on the phone.

Holding her breath, she waited a couple of seconds to see if he was going to call back and ask who or what had taken possession of the rational woman he knew. When he'd had plenty of time to look up her number and the phone didn't ring, she let out a sigh of relief and finished getting dressed. The ribbed gray sweater matched the stitching on her jeans.

Catching a glimpse of herself in her dresser mirror, Phyllis was surprised to see her belly protruding a little. Dr. Mac had apparently seen signs of the baby, but Phyllis hadn't really been able to tell. She was just under twelve weeks along.

She looked more closely, feeling comforted when she could definitely detect a thickening shape she'd never seen before. Fat was soft and ugly. Phyllis's belly, while still perfectly normal to anyone who wasn't studying it, was firm and ever so slightly rounded.

Six weeks ago she'd been lamenting the fact that this pregnancy was going to make her put on the weight she'd painstakingly lost over the past year. Suddenly she couldn't wait.

What on earth was happening to her?

Shaking her head, Phyllis turned off her bedroom light and decided to sort through the mail she'd left on the table in the foyer. She should probably pay bills that night. And maybe start looking more seriously at her long-term financial plans.

She wasn't sure she'd be able to sit still and concentrate. Nervous energy sped through her, making her feel as though she'd consumed a liter of soda loaded with caffeine. She wasn't going to start hemorrhaging. Logically she knew that. She trusted Dr. Mac.

She'd had an exam two days before.

And still she was nervous.

It was Wednesday night. What would Cassie be doing? Or Tory? Or Becca? They'd all be with their husbands; that was a given. Except maybe Cassie. Her friend could be staying late at the clinic. It didn't happen very often anymore, but occasionally it did.

She dialed the veterinary clinic by heart, too. And

listened to the answering machine pick up after the fourth ring. Damn. Cassie was the person she needed. She was the only one Phyllis could talk to about the strange emotions consuming her. Cassie was still the only one who knew that Phyllis was pregnant.

Other than Matt, of course.

There was no way Phyllis was going to call Cassie at home during dinnertime. She'd be sitting at the table with Sam and Mariah and her in-laws, too. They'd all watch her leave the room to answer the phone. Wait for her return. Ask who she'd been talking to...

The Valley Diner downtown was always an option. The food was great. At this time of night there'd be lots of people, friendly conversation, diversion.

Wednesday was chicken enchilada night. Phyllis's mouth was watering already. She'd just put the mail on her desk in the corner of the living room, grab her keys and go.

And if, after dinner, she was still at loose ends, she'd stop by and see Tory and Ben. Alex would still be up, so it wouldn't be as though Phyllis was really interrupting—

Her doorbell rang.

Who could that be? Becca maybe? Dropping something by for another of her committees? Phyllis was one of Becca's best volunteers, with no family making demands on her spare time.

Hurrying to the door before Becca assumed she wasn't home and left, Phyllis decided to tell her friend about the baby. Becca would understand. Hell, when the two women had first met the summer before, Becca had been in the last trimester of a very trying pregnancy herself. Her first baby at forty-two.

They'd become fast friends. Remembering the weeks they'd spent so much time together, weeks when Becca had been separated from the love of her life—her husband, Will, Phyllis's boss—Phyllis knew that Becca was just the person she needed tonight.

Her smile went from overbright to nervous when she saw who was on her step.

"I can't believe you came all the way over here," she said to Matt, standing on the other side of the closed screen door.

"You called."

"I told you I was fine."

"You of all people wouldn't have called if you were fine."

He had her there.

"I was just…having a moment," she said, trying for a careless grin. She didn't think she'd entirely pulled it off. She could feel her bottom lip trembling. "I'm fine now."

She had to get out of there. Get downtown, where she'd be surrounded by people before she had a full-blown panic attack over nothing.

Standing there with his hands in the pockets of his

jeans, Matt could have been posing for a cigarette commercial. Or, more in keeping with the times, a commercial for a rugged off-road vehicle.

"Since I drove all the way over here, why don't you come on out for a second and tell me about this moment you were having?"

She'd opened the door before she'd considered the question. There was no reason to tell him. Nothing to be gained by sharing her ups and downs with him.

But it was so sweet of him to have driven all this way when she knew he really wanted nothing to do with her or the baby.

She sat on the top step, irrationally glad when Matt sat down beside her. *Sure beats the Valley Diner.* But only because she was still too shaky to be keeping up appearances with so many people at once.

Here at home, there was only one person to fool.

And here at home, she was close to her bathroom. Just in case.

"I bled a little bit more today." Phyllis was shocked to hear the words. She knew better than to get close to Matt Sheffield.

But he was the only person who knew about the other day. He'd been at the hospital with her, experienced the entire ordeal. Telling him seemed so natural.

Elbows on his knees, head facing the ground, Matt gave her a sideways glance. "I take it, since we're sitting here, that you're okay?"

"I'm fine."

"Forgive me if I shouldn't be saying this, but you don't sound fine."

"I—"

He sat up, assessed her more completely. "You don't look fine, either."

"Thanks for the compliment," she said dryly. And why had she thought, for even a second, that she wanted to talk with him?

"That's not what I meant," Matt said, frowning. "You look beautiful, of course. But you've also got a crease between your brows and you haven't smiled a genuine smile since I arrived."

"You've been here all of two minutes."

He didn't say anything to that. Just sat there, gazing down the steps in front of them.

Phyllis took in a lungful of fresh, soothing air.

"It's odd, you know," she said slowly. "In the past few years, I haven't imagined myself as a mother, having a baby. I'm always the aunt in the picture."

He glanced at her silently.

"And I was okay with that," she told him. "I really was happy."

"I'm sorry to have ruined all that."

"I thought I was, too. Until today."

Brows raised, he waited for her to continue.

"I mean, as soon as I knew I was pregnant, I wanted the baby. Don't get me wrong. I just thought

I wanted it because I couldn't *not* have it. Because it was mine.''

He looked away, his eyes following a blue SUV as it drove slowly past.

"But suddenly, today, I *have* to have this baby."

"I don't quite understand," Matt said, his gaze returning to her.

"I mean," she said, "a great part of my happiness now rests with this baby."

"How so?" He sounded more curious than anything else.

"Because I'm never going to marry, I assumed that meant I was going to live my life alone." She shook her head. "I don't know why I never considered single parenting before now. It's not like it's all that uncommon these days. And I've got lots of men in my life, friends, to provide a male influence." She shrugged. "I suppose my background was just too conventional for me to make the leap."

"I don't guess there are too many artificial inseminations in Shelter Valley."

"No." She shared a grin with him. "It's a pretty traditional place."

"So you aren't angry about the baby?"

"Hell, no!" Phyllis said, sending him a truly shocked look. "I was never angry."

"My mother would've been furious," he said.

"It never even entered my mind to be angry. Panicked, yes. Unsettled, nervous, scared, even a little depressed. But not angry.'' She thought a moment, and then, ''How about you? Are you angry?''

''At myself, maybe, for doing this to you.''

''But you didn't *do* anything to me.''

His mouth twisted in a fully masculine smirk. ''I think Dr. Mac would disagree with you on that.''

Phyllis blushed, looked down at the steps and then grinned. ''As I recall the, uh, activity that got us here was definitely mutual.''

''I should've known that condom couldn't possibly be safe.''

''Have you spent your whole life doing this?'' Phyllis asked curiously. She liked having him there beside her. He brought warmth to the chilly evening air.

''Doing what?''

''Blaming yourself for things you couldn't possibly have helped.''

Matt was quiet for a few long minutes. ''I could've had a little more control that day we were…together. Stopped things before they got so out of hand.''

''I suppose so. Though the same could be said for me.''

''Have you been doing this all your life?'' he asked, sending her a sideways grin. It was a grin that reached his dark eyes. It was the first time she'd seen that happen.

''Doing what?'' she asked, unable to look away from that gleam in his eyes.

"Taking guilt away from people."

"Is that what I'm doing?"

"I hope so. It sure feels like it."

"Is it working?"

"I don't know yet. But maybe."

She hoped so. He was a good man. And far too hard on himself. He was blaming himself for giving her the one thing she'd never have sought for herself. The one thing that had been missing from her happiness. A family of her own.

She'd feel much better about their association if she could somehow help him find a measure of happiness, too. Help him come to terms with whatever was haunting him.

"I was just on my way down to the diner for chicken enchiladas," she said casually. "Want to join me?"

He took too long to answer her. She knew that whatever answer he gave her wasn't going to be the one he wanted to give.

She wished she hadn't asked.

"No," he finally said, standing. "I should get home and chlorinate the pool."

Phyllis wondered if that was a man's version of having to "wash my hair." But she didn't mind. He really wanted to go with her.

Which meant that, for both their sakes, he'd answered her invitation correctly.

"Sounds fun," she said, standing up beside him. "See ya."

In control once again, she went back inside for her keys. Maybe she'd pick up dessert for Ben and Tory and Alex while she was at the diner. Tory had been craving apple cobbler throughout her entire pregnancy.

And no one made apple cobbler like the Valley Diner.

She waited until Matt had driven away before she locked up and headed out herself. She was glad he was gone.

But she wondered, as she drove downtown, if there was anything Matt Sheffield craved.

And she wondered why finding out suddenly mattered so much.

CHAPTER EIGHT

SHE WAS AN AMAZING WOMAN. An amazing person. Somehow Phyllis Langford had taken a situation he could in no way be proud of—an unplanned, illegitimate pregnancy—and made it a good thing. Made him feel like he'd scaled a mountain. How could he completely hate himself for getting her pregnant when it turned out she wanted the baby so badly?

Instead of ruining her life, he'd somehow bettered it.

Matt walked across campus Thursday afternoon, the collar of his maroon leather jacket lifted up around his neck to ward off the unusual chill. The temperature would be back in the seventies the next day. As soon as the sun came out again. In the meantime, he, like probably the majority of Arizonans, was enjoying the rare cool day.

If he didn't hurry, he was going to miss her. Phyllis only had another fifteen minutes of her office hour. And he wanted to assure himself that she was okay. *Needed* to assure himself.

She wanted this baby. And suddenly he was filled with a forceful determination to do everything in his power to see that she had it. He intended to reestablish the tentative truce he'd made with himself in Shelter Valley.

He'd see her through the pregnancy and in doing so, provide a way to slip back into the life he'd built before he met her. No harm done.

Her door was open. A student just leaving.

"Thanks, Dr. Langford."

"Anytime, Steve." She sounded as though she was smiling.

Matt felt a little like smiling, too.

"Hey, teach, how you doing?" he asked, appearing in her doorway as soon as the student was a couple of doors down the hall. He didn't give her time to get involved in anything he'd have to interrupt.

"Matt?" She was frowning, looking up from a typed paper, red pen in her hand. "What's up?"

Casual visits aren't in our agreement, Matt translated. He was a bit relieved by the message. He wanted to give her every ounce of his strength to bring a healthy baby into the world, but he didn't want to give her any false ideas.

He closed the door behind him, noting the wary look in her eyes. "Have you had any more bleeding?" he asked softly, moving closer to her desk.

Her gaze cleared and she put down the pen. "No," she told him, open now. "I've been nervous all day, but there's nothing. Thank God."

Apparently talk about the baby was okay with her. They both understood that they were on a common mission that had everything to do with this baby and nothing to do with the two of them.

"How about morning sickness? Is that gone, too?"

"I didn't get *that* lucky," she said with a grimace.

"But you're getting enough fluids like Dr. Mac said?"

"Yes, sir." She was smiling at him. And then she frowned again. "Why do you care so much all of a sudden?" she asked sharply. "You aren't getting ideas about this baby, are you?"

"Of course not." He set her mind at rest immediately. "Not for myself, if that's what you mean."

Phyllis sat back, her forearms resting casually on the sides of her padded leather executive desk chair—identical to the one his butt spent so much time in at the Performing Arts Center. "Sorry about that," she said. "I can't believe how often I'm flying off in crazy directions these days. I'll sure be glad when this phase of the pregnancy passes."

"Just to set the record straight—" he placed his hands on her desk, met her gaze head-on "—you have nothing to fear from me. My life is exactly how I want it. I have no interest in close personal relationships, nor am I ever going to foist myself on a kid who, as I know firsthand, would be better off without me."

"You've said that before."

He nodded. "I mean it."

"Why?"

The question hit him between the eyes. He'd lowered his guard, left himself unprotected without even knowing it. Open to the kinds of questions he didn't allow people to ask.

"I told you before. I have a past."

"Hate to break this to you, Matt, but everyone who's lived for more than about a second has a past."

He backed up, didn't meet her eyes. "Yeah, well, mine wouldn't sit well with a kid."

"So why are you here?"

"Because I made you pregnant," he said, leaning on the desk again. "I have a proposition of sorts to run by you."

"What?" She picked up her pen,

"We both need something."

"We do." It wasn't a question, and yet the words were filled with challenge.

"You need that baby."

"Yeeaahhh."

"And I need to feel like I'm doing something to take responsibility, to be accountable, for my part in this whole thing."

"Okay." The word was far too hesitant to be the agreement it implied.

"So I propose that we team up, just for the duration of the pregnancy. I'll be your assistant—be there to do things for you. Not just the heavy things, but whatever needs to be done so you don't get worn-out to the point of needing hospitalization. Dr.

Mac said this morning sickness might continue throughout the pregnancy, you work full-time—something's got to give.''

''But I'm—''

''Most woman have a man at home to step in and tend to the little things while they're pregnant.''

''Yes, but—''

''So, you let me do that—do my part—and in the end, you get the healthy baby you want so badly.''

''And what makes you think we can have an arrangement like this without getting involved in each other's lives?''

''Because neither of us wants involvement. We're immune.''

She frowned. ''I'm a psychologist, Matt. Things don't work that way.''

''Okay, try this, Doc. Because I'm incapable of involvement.''

It shouldn't have hurt when she nodded. Her agreement was exactly what he wanted. And yet, in a small sense, it did hurt. So a woman trained to know about people, their minds and emotions, believed him when he said he was incapable of having a close relationship. It wasn't anything he hadn't already known.

''I can't believe I'm doing this,'' she said, ''but I'm agreeing to your proposition.''

''Good.''

''There are going to be problems here, I just know it.''

"Maybe not."

"There will be."

"So why are you agreeing to it?"

"Because it's the best option. No one but Cassie knows I'm pregnant, and I think I want to keep it that way for as long as I can. At least until I'm sure everything's really okay with this bleeding. It'll just be easier not to have everyone worrying over me. I'm doing enough of that myself."

"I'm not a worrier," he said with a half grin, trying to reassure her the best he could.

"Somehow I knew that about you." She grinned back, her head lowered slightly as she looked at him.

"Anyway, without anyone else knowing, it'd be a little hard at this point to ask for help and not have them wondering what's going on."

"I can see that."

"So—" She stood up, dropping her pen again "—we're a team, we keep this between ourselves for now, we know the ground rules."

"Right."

"Great."

"Good."

"Well…" She stood there watching him as if waiting for something.

"Yeah, well, see ya," he said, turned and left.

He was glad that was done.

"Aunt Phyllis? Do macaronis grow in the ground?"

Phyllis looked across her kitchen table at the sweet

little girl, Tory and Ben's adopted daughter, sitting there shoveling homemade macaroni-and-cheese into her mouth.

"No, Alex," she said, hiding a smile behind her full fork. "They're man-made, but from wheat that grows in the ground."

Her short blond hair giving her an elfin look, Alex stared at the macaroni currently stuck to the end of her fork, her face screwed up in a frown. "What about the cheese part?"

"It's made from milk, which comes from—"

"Cows!" Alex burst out.

"That's right," Phyllis said just as a knock sounded on her back door. She was smiling as she rose to answer it, remembering not so long ago when little Alex had first come to them, a tough little girl who'd been hurt badly. The curious, precocious child sitting at her table now bore little resemblance to the abused and frightened child she'd been less than a year ago. Ben—who'd raised Alex from birth and then lost her to her biological father on his release from prison—had brought her home from California with the approval of state authorities. Ben was her true father, and under his care and Tory's, Alex had regained her confidence.

Until Matt walked into the kitchen. The little blond dynamo froze in her chair, eyes glued on Matt. She stared only until he looked at her and then her eyes dropped. As did her chin. And her fork.

"Come here, munchkin," Phyllis said, sitting down at the table again and pulling Alex out of her chair and onto her lap. "I want you to meet a friend of mine. This is Matt. Matt, this is Alex."

The two eyed each other, and Phyllis, watching them, could see wariness in both faces.

"Hi, Alex," Matt said, his voice friendly, giving no indication of the hesitation Phyllis had just read in his expression.

Alex said nothing. Just continued to stare.

"Alex is Ben and Tory's daughter," Phyllis said. Matt nodded.

"She's having dinner with me tonight while Ben and Tory attend Lamaze class."

"Well, your dinner sure looks good," he said, his tone obviously meant to put the little girl at ease.

As Matt crouched by the cupboard that held her cleaning supplies, Alex wrapped her arms around Phyllis's neck, drawing her head down.

"He's a good guy?" she whispered, her face only an inch from Phyllis's, her look intent.

"He's a good guy," Phyllis whispered back, sending an apologetic glance toward Matt. She'd told him about Tory's past. But hadn't told him about the special, intimate bond Tory shared with her new daughter, the bond of abuse the two of them had suffered. Both had been damaged by those given the charge of keeping them safe. "I wouldn't let anyone near you who wasn't a good guy, don't you know that?" Phyllis continued softly, giving the child a hug.

After a moment of thought, Alex nodded, slid off Phyllis's lap, and climbed onto her own chair to finish her dinner. Life was normal again.

Phyllis wished it was always that easy.

"I teach at Montford. And I work on plays there." Matt told the child, stopping on his way out of the kitchen, a bottle of drain cleaner in his hand. "Maybe you can see one sometime."

"Where Mommy and Daddy go to school?" Alex asked him. She didn't bother to look up from her dinner.

"Yep."

"Cool."

On that vote of approval, Matt turned to Phyllis. "I noticed the drain in your guest bathroom sink was running a little slow. I'll take care of that and check the other ones, as well. You shouldn't be inhaling this stuff."

"Thanks," Phyllis said. She was talking to his back. He'd already left the room.

"Aunt Phyllis? When Mommy has the baby, will it hurt?" Alex was asking when Matt walked back into the kitchen several minutes later.

"Just for a little while," Phyllis answered, trying to keep her mind on the conversation and off the man who'd just entered the room. Time with Alex was filled with a barrage of unexpected questions that could only come from an introspective seven-year-old. She required full attention.

"Then how come Daddy's letting her have one? He told us he'd never let anything hurt us again."

Matt coughed.

"Because the baby will make your mommy so happy she won't care about a little bit of pain."

"How come babies can't be born without hurting their moms?" Alex asked around a mouthful of macaroni. She'd never noticed before what an inordinately slow eater the child was. Alex hadn't even started on her carrots and peas.

Sending her a commiserating grin behind the girl's back, Matt excused himself to check a sprinkler head. He claimed it had been spraying straight up when he'd pulled into the drive.

Chicken, Phyllis called silently after him.

AFTER HE'D REPLACED the sprinkler valve, Matt carried Phyllis's laundry in from the bedroom and was ready to go.

"Won't you have some dinner?" Phyllis asked. "It's only macaroni-and-cheese with vegetables, but there's plenty of it."

"Aunt Phyllis makes the not-from-a-box kind," Alex told him importantly. Phyllis was astonished to see how quickly the little girl had relaxed around him. With just the brief exchange they'd shared earlier, she appeared to be as unconcerned about him as she was with Sam or Will or any other of "her" people in Shelter Valley.

Was it a sign of the healing power of love that

was found in Shelter Valley in such abundance? Or something Matt himself had done?

Matt ruffled the little girl's hair. "If I hadn't already eaten, I'd take you up on that," he said. "Tasty, isn't it?"

"It's the best," Alex told him. "Just like Aunt Phyllis."

Meeting her eyes over the little girl's head, Matt's eyes were suddenly serious. "You're right about that."

WHEN MATT CAME OVER on Friday after work, Phyllis wasn't even surprised to see him.

Tonight he was wearing a pair of faded jeans with holes in the knees and an old T-shirt with writing so faded she couldn't make out what it said. It was fifty degrees outside and he didn't even have a coat on.

"I really don't need anything tonight," she said, following him out to the kitchen. "I've got a pan of frozen lasagna in the oven for dinner, which is light enough for me to lift out myself after it's cooked another hour, and then I'm going to soak in the tub and go to bed and read."

He nodded. "I won't get in your way."

Hadn't he heard her? He wasn't needed here. It was Friday night and Phyllis was planning to spoil herself, think about her baby—and enjoy not having to struggle through the traditional Friday-night blues as everyone else went home to families and she faced another batch of weekend chores alone. She wasn't alone anymore. She'd be doing her Saturday cleaning for two. And grocery-shopping, too. Especially grocery-shopping, since Dr. Mac had her on a special high protein and glucose diet.

Matt got cleaning supplies from the cupboard under the sink.

"What are you doing?"

"You told me that night in the hospital that you clean on Saturday mornings. I have to be at the theater in the morning."

"So?"

"So I'm doing it tonight, instead." He stopped. "Unless you have someone coming over to soak in that tub with you...?"

"Of course not!" She felt her entire body turning red at the thought. She was *pregnant,* for God's sake.

And with his child, no less.

"Then I'd best get started," he said.

"But—"

"I know I'm probably not going to do things exactly as you're used to." He sprayed some furniture polish on a rag and headed into the living room.

Phyllis followed him.

"But you don't have to worry," he continued as he carefully removed everything from her coffee table. "I don't like dirt, and since I live alone, I've learned how to handle a pretty mean rag."

As he spoke, he wiped not only the top of the coffee table, but the legs and sides, then returned everything to its original place. If the man ever lost his job at the university, he could open a cleaning service.

Because she was practically speechless—and because she enjoyed watching him efficiently and thoroughly move his gorgeous body around her living room—Phyllis just stood there for the next few minutes. He polished all the furniture, including the sofa legs. And the picture frames on the mantel.

"I can dust," she finally said when he'd almost finished the room. She figured she should do *something*. It was her house, after all.

"We agreed—"

"That you'd help me," she said, finding the will to assert herself. "Not that you'd turn me into an invalid. I'll dust, you vacuum and we can be done with this by the time the lasagna's done."

"You dust, I'll vacuum and scrub the bathrooms—"

"While I do the kitchen sink and countertops."

He looked at her for a moment. "Agreed," he eventually said, "on the condition that you leave mopping the kitchen floor to me and that you stop as soon as you start to feel tired."

Phyllis grinned. "I'm pregnant, Sheffield, not old."

She wasn't positive, because he was turning away to get to work, but Phyllis thought he grinned back at her.

AFTER CHANGING into a pair of jeans that weren't too tight yet, Phyllis did a quick check of her bathroom to make sure there wasn't anything too personal or embarrassing lying out. Everything was in its proper drawer or cupboard.

Matt vacuumed the living room while she dusted the bedroom. She took care of the towel racks, toiletries and knickknacks in both bathrooms while he vacuumed her bedroom.

Odd, having a man in her bedroom after so many years. Odder still having him in there cleaning.

She moved on to the spare bedroom—imagining the nursery it was soon to become, the baby who'd be living there—while he did the bathrooms. And then she moved on to the kitchen.

She was still working on the counters when he came in to do the floors. She wiped, he swept. The smell of the cooking lasagna filled the room. She actually felt hungry.

"I've hardly ever met a man comfortable enough with himself to do 'women's work' so unselfconsciously." Phyllis hadn't really meant to speak her thoughts aloud.

Matt shrugged and then bent to position the dustpan. Holding the brush easily between fingers and thumb, he swept up the crumbs that had been on the floor. "That's the beauty of being alone. I've got no one to impress, so no reason to be self-conscious."

"Most people spend a lot of their time trying to impress themselves." She finished wiping and leaned against the counter, watching him fill a bucket with water. He splashed in just the right amount of pine-scented disinfectant, wrung out the mop as he'd done this countless times before and methodically set to work on the floor.

"I already know what I'm made of," he said after a few swipes. "No point trying to kid myself now."

"You're secure with who you are," she said. It impressed her—and he didn't seem to be trying.

He mopped.

The buzzer went off, signaling that the lasagna was done. Reaching for a towel from the rack, Phyllis stepped on it and slid her way over to the oven.

"How much more have you got to do?" she asked him. She didn't think he'd vacuumed the spare bedroom yet. He'd brought out the mop for the bathroom floors and continued right into the kitchen with it.

"Just some vacuuming."

"Why not stop long enough to have some dinner, then?" she asked, trying not to feel nervous about the invitation. There was something so…intimate about having him sit down to a meal with her at her own table.

"There's more here than I'm going to eat," she added when he said nothing.

He glanced over at the sizzling pan as she pulled it out of the oven. "I might have a bite or two," he said. "But I have to finish up here first. You go ahead."

She did. Partially because, with the floor mostly

wet, it was easier just to fill a plate and sit at the table and out of his way. And partially because she really was hungry, for the first time in weeks.

Matt finished mopping, rinsed the mop and bucket, put his supplies away. And then helped himself to a huge portion of lasagna, using the plate she'd left out on the counter for him. Grabbing a fork from the cutlery drawer, he leaned back against the kitchen counter and ate.

It was so nonthreatening, not really eating together at all, that Phyllis relaxed again. Maybe he was right. Maybe they really could make this work.

"How's your star student been this week?" she asked him when the silence began to feel awkward. He'd told her about Sophie on Monday, but nothing since.

He shrugged, eating attentively. "About the same. I've seen her a few times, but she still isn't as sharp as normal. It's odd—she'll be fine, and then just seem to lose her concentration."

Grateful for the diversion—and also because it was her nature to try to solve emotional problems—Phyllis went to work.

"You said she's lost weight," she said, running through everything he'd told her about the girl. "Would you say she's lost too much weight, or she's just taking care of herself?"

"Definitely too much weight," he said, slowing a moment to glance over at her. "Her cheekbones are

stark. If she were any older, her skin would be hanging on her.''

"Does she seem to talk about food much?"

Matt stopped eating altogether, apparently thinking back over recent conversations with the girl.
"Maybe," he said. "Yeah, I guess. I can think of
several times she's mentioned it, and since we don't
talk all that much, I guess she must mention it a lot.''

"And you said she's wearing bulky clothes.''

"Yeah.''

Phyllis remembered something else, something
he'd commented on while they were at the hospital.
"And she has one fingernail that's broken when all
the others are long?''

"Yeah.''

Anorexia. If Phyllis hadn't been so distracted the
other night, she would've put all the symptoms together then. Of course, the disease was usually only
a symptom of some bigger emotional problem.

"Have you noticed the hair on her arms?'' she
asked Matt, not sure he'd welcome her suspicions.

"No, of course not!'' He set his empty plate on
the counter. "Why would you ask that?''

"Because it sounds to me like she has an eating
disorder, and one sign of the more advanced stages
is body hair turning to fuzz. It's pretty distinctive if
you know what you're looking for.''

"I haven't seen Sophie's arms in ages. She's always wearing sweaters or sweatshirts. Not that I'd

notice something like that if I did see them. What makes you think she has an eating disorder?''

He obviously wasn't thrilled with the diagnosis.

He cared about the girl.

Finishing her own dinner, Phyllis checked to see that the floor was dry enough and walked her plate over to the sink. ''The fingernail is a pretty clear indication.''

''Come on, Doc,'' Matt said. ''Fingernails do break.''

''And there are many ways a girl can take care of that nowadays. Even if she doesn't have the time or money for a proper manicure, she can buy glue-on tips at the drugstore. If Sophie's as particular about her nails as you described, there has to be a damn good reason for her to keep that one short.''

''And what reason would that be?''

''So she can stick her finger down her throat to throw up after she eats.''

Standing beside her, he rinsed his own plate and handed it to her to put in the dishwasher. He didn't say anything.

''If she is anorexic or bulimic, she needs help, Matt.''

''I teach lighting design.''

''But you said she came to you for guidance.''

''I teach lighting design.''

''I realize that!'' Phyllis said, wishing he'd let her past the barriers he'd erected. ''So you don't know about eating disorders, but you know about people. And she trusts you.''

''There's nothing I can do.''

''You can at least try to get her to talk to someone, to see a counselor.''

''I'll suggest it on Monday,'' he said, and then, ''I'm going to finish that vacuuming and leave you to your bath and your book. I'll be back tomorrow afternoon to take you grocery-shopping. Thanks for dinner.''

Before she could say, ''You're welcome,'' he was gone.

Probably just as well. He could clean for her. Take out her trash. Stand at her kitchen counter and eat.

He couldn't be welcome in her life.

CHAPTER NINE

MATT FELT A LITTLE AWKWARD. Okay, he felt damn stupid. It wasn't that he wasn't used to grocery-shopping, pushing a cart up and down the aisles, filling it with stuff. He did all that. Regularly. But he'd never pushed a cart being filled with stuff for someone else. He was finding out more than he needed to know about Phyllis Langford.

Her tastes in food. What brand of toilet paper she used. What kind of toothpaste.

"You know, those would be cheaper at Wal-Mart," he told her when she added paper towels and tissues to the cart. She'd chosen the same brands he used.

A Wal-Mart had opened on the outskirts of town two years before.

"I know." She nodded, and continued loading the cart. "I just figured it was worth the few cents I'd have saved not to drag you to another place."

"I have to go, anyway."

She glanced back at him, the first time she'd met his eyes fully since he'd picked her up half an hour earlier. "Maybe next week, then." Her focus returned to the list she'd been concentrating on.

She looked great. The tight beige hip-huggers she was wearing with a black chenille turtleneck sweater were practical and sexy as hell at the same time. Hard to believe, looking at her, that she was pregnant.

Feminine and baby items were in the next row. Phyllis eyed the baby items, pausing as though she'd like to linger, ran a hand through her windblown hair, but pressed on. She stopped in front of the feminine supplies.

Matt studied the baby items. There were a lot of different pacifiers. One claimed that it was orthodontically tested. Matt was glad to see that.

Phyllis slid a small bag of feminine napkins onto the underside of the basket, next to the toilet paper.

"You bleeding again?" he asked.

She shot him a startled look, glanced around. He'd made her uncomfortable.

Damn. "Sorry."

"No." She glanced back quickly and then away. "I mean, it's a little late to feel embarrassed after you spent all that time with me at the hospital, listening to Dr. Mac's thorough diagnosis."

Her shyness made him a little tight in the jeans.

And that wasn't supposed to happen, either. He pulled his black leather jacket closed, fastening the bottom of the zipper.

They moved on.

"I had a little more spotting this morning," Phyllis said out of the blue as she walked slowly down the cereal aisle. The store was crowded—as it always was on a Saturday afternoon in Shelter Valley—but it still seemed as though they were in a world of their own.

"Just this morning?" he asked, his stomach heavy. The doctor had said not to worry if there was more spotting, but he'd feel a hell of a lot better if it just stopped happening to Phyllis.

"Yeah," she said, taking a box of cereal off the shelf. "I called Dr. Mac's office, though. She sees patients for a couple of hours on Saturday mornings, so I knew she'd be in."

"And?"

Phyllis hesitated, her expressive green eyes shaded from him. "She thinks I overdid things last night with the cleaning," she admitted, though grudgingly.

"I'm glad she agrees with me."

Phyllis finally looked at him. "You didn't argue with me last night."

"I knew better."

She held his gaze for another second and then turned away, grabbing a box of granola bars.

"You know those are filled with sugar."

"Carbohydrates are good for me."

"But if you got some kind of energy bar, you'd have the carbs and a large supply of vitamins, as well."

"Yeah, and they taste like crap. Besides, I'm on horse-pill vitamins. I don't think I need any more."

He wondered if crankiness came with the territory,

or if this was just a side of Phyllis he hadn't seen before.

He kind of liked it. The intelligent doctor wasn't perfect.

Deciding to keep his mouth closed for the remainder of the shopping trip, Matt amused himself by watching her at work. She took her shopping very seriously. Comparing prices, checking things off her list.

In the dairy section she took a quart of milk from the refrigerated glass enclosure.

"It's much cheaper by the gallon," he said, forgetting his intention to mind his own business.

"Not if you don't use a gallon," she told him, putting the quart in the cart. "I hate milk. I'm only buying it because Dr. Mac told me I should have at least one glass a day. I'm figuring that's the best I'll be able to do."

Matt loved milk. He went through a couple of gallons a week. Now probably wasn't the time to say so.

"I saw Sophie today," he said, instead. He'd promised himself he'd talk to the girl about her situation, but only to get it off his own shoulders.

"How was she?"

"More talkative," he told her. He'd actually been encouraged by that, if not by the rest of what he had to report. "She did have fuzzy arms, though. Of course, that just might be how her hair grows. It's not like I ever looked before, so I have nothing to compare it to.''

Phyllis shook her head. ''I suspect there's a problem,'' she said, her brow lined.

''I asked her to see a counselor.'' Matt strolled along beside her, approving of her rice and pasta choices. Even the spaghetti sauce, about which he was rather particular.

''Did she say she would?''

''No.''

On the contrary, she'd fought him adamantly. Said some other stuff that had made his jaw tense. As long as she had him to talk to, she didn't need anyone else. He understood her. She trusted him. Stuff like that.

He didn't want her trust.

''She says she doesn't need the help,'' he murmured.

''Yet she comes to you.''

''Yeah.'' And it was really bothering him. He hadn't felt so trapped since he'd been locked up in a ten-by-ten cell.

''You need to keep trying, Matt,'' Phyllis said emphatically. They were moving toward the checkout. ''If you're the only one she's talking to, you might be her only hope. Stick close to her, gain her confidence. Maybe you'll convince her to change her mind.''

''Not likely.''

He couldn't do that, couldn't let her get any closer.

Sophie was already much too close for his comfort. Damn thing was, she was a great kid, with more potential than any student he'd had since coming to Montford, and Montford, with its small enrollment and impressive reputation, brought in only the best.

"If you think it'll help, I'd be glad to come and talk to her," Phyllis offered.

Unloading the groceries onto the counter for her— heavy items first, light items last so when they rolled down to be bagged, nothing would be smashed or damaged—Matt considered the idea. He wasn't sure he liked it—adding another knot to the tangle that his relationship with Phyllis had become. But he sure wanted to back away from his involvement with the pretty coed.

"I just might take you up on that, Doc," he told Phyllis, "if you're sure it's not too much trouble."

"Not at all. I'd like to help. It's what I do."

Matt nodded; he already knew that about her.

"Besides," Phyllis continued, moving up to the cashier as she finished emptying the basket and pushed it down toward the bag boy. "It'd be a way I can repay you for all the work you're doing."

"Uh, I'm the one in debt here," he said, glancing pointedly at her stomach.

Her little grimace grabbed his gut and wouldn't let go.

"Phyllis?"

Coming fully awake, hardly aware of how she'd

come to have the phone at her ear, Phyllis sat up in bed.

What time is it? "Tor? What's up, honey?"

Three o'clock in the morning. Phyllis tensed. Three o'clock in the morning could mean only one thing, and it wasn't time for that yet. Tory had another month to go.

"My water broke," the younger woman said. "Can you come?"

"I'm on my way," Phyllis said, taking the phone with her as she pulled on the beige slacks and black sweater she'd worn grocery shopping with Matt the day before. "Have you called the Montfords?"

Ben Sanders, Tory's husband, was out of town with his daughter, Alex, that weekend, finalizing his sole custody of the child, as her mother was signing away all rights. He was Sam Montford's cousin, the elder Montfords' nephew, something they'd only discovered the year before, when Ben had come to Shelter Valley to start his life over. Which meant the Montfords were Tory's family now.

"No," Tory said. "I just want you."

Phyllis could hear the panic in Tory's voice. The whole reason Ben had gone to California now—taking Alex out of school—was that he'd thought the time was safe. He hadn't wanted to wait and go during Alex's Christmas break. He'd figured that was too risky, cutting it too close.

"How far apart are the pains?" Phyllis asked, slipping into black ankle boots.

"Seven minutes."

Phyllis nodded. Okay, that was good. "You have a bag packed?" she asked next, intending to keep her friend on the phone until she could get to her.

"Yeah."

"And you've called the hospital?"

"Yeah."

"Okay." Phyllis grabbed her keys, her purse, pulling out her cell phone. "You have call waiting, right?" she asked.

"Yeah."

Phyllis dialed the number quickly. "Pick up when it beeps," she said.

Tory did. And as Phyllis sped the few short blocks to the pretty little house Ben and Tory had bought from Randi Parsons the previous spring, she kept Tory distracted. Kept her talking.

It was a long night. The drive into Phoenix seemed endless. Throughout the trip, she was helping Tory breathe through the pains that continued to come at regular seven minute intervals all the way from Shelter Valley to the hospital. It was an even longer day on Sunday. Tory dilated to eight centimeters and stopped. She needed to get to ten. And though she was no longer making progress, the contractions, instead of lessening, only heightened in intensity.

Phyllis had been trying to get hold of Ben most of the morning, first from the cell phone in her car and then using the phone in Tory's room. But by midafternoon she'd still been unable to reach him.

The phone line to the motel where Ben was staying was busy every time Phyllis got a chance to call, and by the time she'd realized the number was wrong— two figures were reversed—and got the right one, Ben had already checked out. He was presumably on his way home—a six-hour drive—but Tory said he'd been planning to take a detour and show Alex the Grand Canyon. She left a message for him at the house.

"He needs a cell phone," Phyllis muttered under her breath. She was across the birthing room from Tory, perched on the edge of a rocking chair that was part of the living-room ensemble set up for family members awaiting the birth. Tory, sweaty and looking ragged, no sign of the eyeliner she always wore, was lying in bed with her eyes closed, but Phyllis knew her friend wasn't asleep.

Why couldn't this, at least, be easy for Tory? Phyllis wondered, hating her helplessness while she watched her friend suffer. The twenty-four-year-old woman had already had far more than her fair share of suffering.

"Phyllis?" Tory's voice was cracked. Dry.

"Yeah, honey, I'm right here." Tory's coloring wasn't good. She seemed too pale, with red blotches on her neck and the exposed upper part of her chest.

"Is something wrong with my baby?"

Tory's eyes were still closed. Phyllis didn't need to see them to picture the shadows that had been back in their depths for the past few hours. It had been months since Phyllis had seen those shadows.

"Everything looks fine, honey," Phyllis said, repeating what the doctor had tentatively reported when Phyllis had followed her out of the room the last time she'd stopped by. The doctor and nurses were in there often, watching all the monitors hooked up to Tory. They were taking extra care, Phyllis knew that. Knew, too, that this could mean they expected a greater chance of something going wrong.

But that was natural, considering Tory was almost a month early.

"It doesn't feel fine."

Phyllis's stomach tensed. "I know, Tor, but I think that's pretty normal. Giving birth is hard work and you're tired."

Tory's eyes opened, pinning Phyllis. "No, I mean it really doesn't feel right."

"How?" Phyllis asked, a sense of urgency filling her. Tory's eyes had a strange look about them. Glazed. Like she was disconnecting from the reality around her.

"Something's...breaking...down there."

Pressing the nurse's call button, Phyllis took Tory's right hand—the one not connected to the intravenous drip—and rubbed it. "You hang in there, Tor," she said, her voice firm. "Everything's going to be okay."

"You need something?" The nurse peeked around the door, took one look at Tory and suddenly all hell broke loose. There were nurses surrounding Tory's bed, checking her blood pressure, taking note of monitor readings, checking Tory's progress. Another minute passed and then Dr. Anderson, Tory's obstetrician, arrived.

Phyllis, staying right by Tory's side while they worked on her, relaxed slightly. Dr. Anderson had been Becca Parsons's doctor and had brought Becca, a forty-two-year-old with a first pregnancy, through a high-risk birth with textbook ease.

"Phyllis?" Tory cried out at one point, flinching, though whether that was from what the doctor was doing or from another contraction, Phyllis couldn't be sure. With all the people around the bed, Phyllis couldn't see the monitor she'd been watching for hours. From it she'd been able to tell when the contractions were coming and how severe they were.

"I'm right here," she told Tory, squeezing the younger woman's fingers.

"It hurts," Tory said.

Phyllis, glancing over at Dr. Anderson, tried to ascertain what was going on, but the doctor was too busy to give her any notice.

"Just hold on, sweetie," Dr. Anderson said then. "You're going to feel some pressure."

Tory moaned.

Holding as tightly as she could to her own fear, Phyllis wiped away the tears that slipped from Tory's closed eyes and slid down her cheeks.

She'd gladly suffer every bit of this for Tory. The

young woman had been through enough. Didn't deserve this, too. Especially not without Ben by her side.

It dawned on Phyllis, as she stood there, trying every calming technique she knew, for herself and for Tory, that she wasn't as far away from Tory's suffering as she'd thought. In a few short months she could be the one lying there, struggling to bring her baby to life....

"The baby's turned and I can't get her to turn back," Dr. Anderson said. "The cord's around her neck. We're going to have to do a C-section before she goes into distress."

"She's okay for now?" Phyllis asked.

"She is."

The doctor's words instilled a confidence Phyllis had badly needed. Dr. Anderson glanced at Tory, who was fading in and out of awareness as the pain racked her body.

"Would you like to stay with her?"

"Yes." Phyllis didn't hesitate for a second. There was no way she was leaving Tory alone if she didn't absolutely have to.

The doctor nodded. "You'll need to get prepped...."

Phyllis followed the nurse Dr. Anderson had pointed out, leaving Tory for only as long as it took to get herself ready. By the time she returned to Tory, wearing scrubs, a mask and gloves, the younger woman looked a little better. Tory's color was back, her face a bit more relaxed. She'd opted to stay awake for the surgery, choosing a local anesthetic rather than a general. They'd already put something for the pain in her IV.

"I sure don't do things by half measures, do I?" Tory asked as Phyllis approached the delivery table and took Tory's free hand in her own. People were working down at the other end of the table, but Dr. Anderson had not yet reappeared.

"You sure don't," Phyllis agreed with a grin, "but you do them very well."

Tory's eyes clouded. "I sure hope so."

"The baby's fine, Tor," Phyllis said insistently. And prayed silently that she was right. God, she wished Ben was there.

"Ben's going to be so mad..." Tory licked her dry lips.

Wishing she had an ice cube to rub along Tory's lips, Phyllis leaned closer, calling up the sternest expression she could.

"You stop right there, Tory Sanders. That man couldn't get mad at you if he tried, he's so damned in love with you."

Tory grinned, a small, weary grin. "I meant he was going to be mad at himself," she whispered. The nurse rubbed a dark orange liquid—antiseptic—over the huge mound of Tory's stomach and even that little bit of pressure was too much. Tory groaned in agony.

The painkiller was working some, but obviously

not enough. Phyllis hoped Dr. Anderson arrived soon—and got this thing over with.

Tory's eyes were starting to look a little wild again.

It went downhill from there. They had to administer the epidural that would numb the lower half of Tory's body for the surgery.

That was difficult, too, and Tory was in so much pain Phyllis wished they'd just knock her out. She insisted one of the nurses do that, but there were procedures to be followed. People to call in.

It would take a minute or two.

They placed a tentlike structure around the lower half of Tory's body, blocking any actual surgical procedure from view.

"I can't do it...."

"Yes, you can." Phyllis's voice was stern, her grip tight on Tory's hand. One of the nurses looked up, concerned.

"The doctor will be here in a second."

"Just let me go, Phyl..." Tory's voice was strong and then faded to nothing. "I'm too tired..."

"You aren't going anywhere," Phyllis said, more scared than she'd ever been in her life. "You hear me?" she demanded, mustering up anger from somewhere. "You hang on, Tory. You have a job to do here."

She'd keep the young woman with her by sheer force of will if she had to. Tory had paid a big price for her happiness. She wasn't going to lose it now. Not if Phyllis had anything to say about it.

CHAPTER TEN

A MONITOR STARTED to beep alarmingly, and hospital personnel scurried. Dr. Anderson came in almost immediately. There wasn't time to put Tory to sleep.

"Let's bring this little girl home, shall we?"

Tory started to cry. Big racking sobs, "I can't, Phyllis. Not without Ben."

"Yes, you can. You've done much worse than this, honey."

And she had. Tory had lain all alone the last time she'd been in a hospital. She'd dealt with great pain and fear then, too—and grief. The car accident that had put her there had killed her beloved older sister.

"If I tell you a secret, do you promise not to tell anyone?" Phyllis asked, desperate for a way to keep Tory with her.

Tory nodded, her pretty blue eyes focusing on Phyllis's face. Phyllis could see the effort it took Tory to do that much and had to choke back her own tears.

"You aren't the only one bringing a baby into the world," she said, moving in close enough to force Tory to meet her eyes.

"I know," Tory croaked. And then, "Cassie and Randi, too." Phyllis could read her friend's weariness on her face. Not just exhaustion from the difficult birth, but from all the struggles life had brought her way.

Somehow they made Phyllis's struggles seem like nothing. Even if something terrible happened and Phyllis lost her baby, she wouldn't have suffered as her young friend had.

"There's someone else, too," Phyllis said, knowing she'd do anything to take Tory's mind off these next minutes as the doctor delivered her baby.

She had a feeling her carefully kept secret would, if nothing else, grab Tory's attention for a second. And even a second away from the fear and the pain would be worth it.

"Who else?" Tory's voice was fading again, her head falling to the side.

"Me."

"What?" Tory asked, her face moving back toward Phyllis.

Phyllis nodded and found a tremulous smile. "I'm three months along as of yesterday."

Tory's tired blue eyes focused completely, searching Phyllis's face. She frowned, obviously concentrating with great effort.

"You're pregnant?"

Dr. Anderson was working swiftly. "Yep," Phyllis said, smiling at Tory.

"Who's...the...father?"

Of course, thought Phyllis. Of course Tory would ask that. She should have expected it. But she hadn't thought things through. She'd been desperately grasping for something to distract Tory from the terror she'd been experiencing.

"Nobody you know," she said. "Nobody I really even know."

Tory's eyes widened, filled with horror. "You weren't—"

"No!" Phyllis said quickly, rubbing Tory's hand between both of hers. "I wasn't raped, Tor," she told her. She should've realized that Tory, with her past, would immediately jump to that conclusion.

"He was just someone I met and had a one-night fling with. And I ended up with a consequence I didn't count on."

Tory flinched.

"Felt that, eh?" Dr. Anderson asked.

"Y-y-yeah," Tory got the word out on the third try.

"Just a couple more minutes," the doctor said cheerily. "We're almost there."

Judging by the intent look on Dr. Anderson's face, as well as on the faces surrounding her, Phyllis wasn't sure the outcome was going to be as cheery as the doctor sounded. But for Tory's sake, she appreciated the older woman's bedside manner.

"D-did, mmm, oowwooo, does he know?" Tory half-whispered, half-cried.

"Yes, he does."

"Almost there," Dr. Anderson said.

"And?" Tory asked breathlessly.

"We have an agreement," Phyllis said, knowing that it was only the situation that would let her get away with an answer so vague. "Get ready, Tor, I think it's time to say hello to your daughter."

Phyllis got just a glimpse of the newborn as Dr. Anderson moved, and then she heard a robust cry of protest.

"Say hello to your mommy," Dr. Anderson said, holding the baby up for one brief moment so Tory could see her. Then she handed the infant to the waiting medical personnel, who whisked her to a nearby table to examine her.

Phyllis didn't know, as she reached down to take Tory in her arms, which of them was sobbing harder.

"You did it, Tor," Phyllis whispered in Tory's ear.

Tory clutched Phyllis desperately, not letting go even as the doctor delivered the afterbirth and stitched her up.

"Thank you, Phyllis," Tory whispered fervently.

"I didn't do anything but stand here, Tor. You did all the work."

"I couldn't have done it without you," Tory said, her voice stronger as she drew back and looked Phyllis straight in the eye. "Not this, not any of it. Thank you for giving me back my life."

Phyllis swallowed a fresh spate of tears. "You're welcome."

"I can see why Christine loved you so much," Tory said, tears dripping slowly down her cheeks.

"I loved her, too, you know."

Tory nodded, turning her head to watch the people working on her daughter.

"I'm naming her Phyllis Christine."

Phyllis couldn't speak after that, too emotional to get any words out. She and Christine together again, in the form of a perfect little baby girl who was destined to bring years and years of long-overdue happiness to the people who'd given her life.

She watched the nurses with the baby, catching sight of a flailing foot, a tiny hand, as they cleaned her up, checking her vitals.

"Sir, sir, you can't just barge in there!"

Phyllis and Tory turned to see a harried-looking Ben, still pulling on a pair of scrubs, come charging into the room.

"Ben!" Tory cried, eyes shining with relief and need.

Ben didn't even notice the baby in the nurse's arms. His eyes went straight to Tory's, searching desperately for reassurance.

"Tory, sweetheart, are you all right?"

Phyllis backed away as Ben stood beside his wife, taking her hand.

"Fine, now that you're here," Tory said.

Dr. Anderson glanced up, smiled at the couple and went silently and efficiently back to work.

"I'm so sorry, love. I should've been here."

Tory's eyes filled with fresh tears. "You were," she said softly. "In my heart, you were here every second."

"Would you like to see your daughter, sir?" a nurse interrupted. She was holding Phyllis Christine, wrapped in a blanket with a tiny pastel-colored cap on her head.

Ben turned toward her, then stopped abruptly. Phyllis found herself crying again as she witnessed Ben's first glimpse of his new daughter. She'd never seen such a look before. Masculine, strong, vigilant—and completely vulnerable at the same time.

Phyllis Christine had a slave for life. One who was going to provide for her, protect her and cherish her in the way only a father could.

Something Phyllis's baby was never going to have.

For the first time, she considered the full ramifications of what she was doing. Simply by the circumstance of her baby's conception and birth, he or she was going to come into the world at a disadvantage.

Her baby wouldn't ever know a father's protection. A father's adoration. Would never have that wealth of unconditional love a good man naturally gave his child.

Choking on the sobs that she could no longer hold back, Phyllis hurried from the room.

WHERE THE HELL was she? Tossing his portable phone on the kitchen counter, Matt looked down at the shining hardwood floors he'd treated that morning, reminding himself that Phyllis Langford was a responsible, capable adult. He should be watching the football game on television, drinking a beer, getting online to place bets with the anonymous friends he'd spent the past couple of years "watching" Sunday afternoon football with. Friends he'd never met.

Instead, he grabbed the keys to his Blazer and locked up the house. He'd helped build the place a couple of years before on the acreage he'd bought just outside Shelter Valley. He headed back into town, back to Phyllis's house. He'd told Phyllis he'd be over when she got home from church; he planned to do anything that needed doing to help her get ready for the coming week. After Saturday, when they'd known that Friday night's cleaning had been too much for her, she'd easily agreed to his offer.

When he'd arrived at her home a couple of hours before, she hadn't been home. And she hadn't answered her phone since.

Sweating by the time he turned onto Phyllis's street—in spite of the fifty-degree weather and the fact that he hadn't turned on the heat in the Blazer—Matt concentrated on separating himself from the situation, stepping outside it. A technique he'd learned during the long days of a court battle that he, a poor young man from a family of convicts, hadn't had a hope of winning.

Phyllis was fine. She would've called if there was

a problem. And if there *was* a problem and she *hadn't* called...well, it was none of his business, anyway. She was nothing to him but an obligation; serving her was simply paying off a debt. Paying what he owed her...

And the baby. He didn't think about that.

Still, though he tried to hide it from himself, the relief Matt felt when he saw Phyllis's car in her drive eased every muscle in his body.

He knocked, impatient when there was no immediate answer. He'd called just a few minutes ago. She couldn't have been home long.

He knocked again, more loudly.

The door opened, but only a crack.

"Oh, Matt, hi," she said, her voice froggy, as though she'd been sleeping. Or crying. "Sorry, I forgot you were coming over."

Good thing he had nothing invested here.

"Did I wake you?" he asked, shrugging off her apology.

"No."

He pulled open the screen door she never locked. "If you'll just open that door a little wider, I'll be able to slide through and get to the trash." He tried for a grin, but was too tense to pull it off. She was acting so out of character....

And then it hit him. Maybe she had a man in there.

Heat sliding up his body, he stepped back as far as he could without actually letting go of the screen door. "Unless you'd rather I came back later..."

What a fool he was. No wonder she hadn't answered her door.

And it wasn't as if she owed him any explanation or needed to inform him when she was entertaining.

There was no reason for him to feel slighted by that, either.

"The trash can wait until tomorrow," she said, sounding weary.

Matt was just about to release the door, go while the going was good. And then she sniffled.

Leaning in, he got a closer look at her, the swollen eyes that suggested she hadn't slept all night. Or that she'd been crying. Or both.

"What's wrong?" he asked, forgetting it wasn't any of his business.

"Nothing. I just…" She might have been striving for an appearance of normalcy, but she failed miserably when she started to cry outright.

Matt pushed gently against the door, joining her in the foyer. "The baby?" He forced the words through a tight throat.

If anything had happened to that child…

"No," Phyllis said, looking up with the first sign of real life in her eyes. "The baby's fine."

The baby might be, but she wasn't. She looked terrible. Her hair was skewed as usual, but not fashionably. Today the waves were haphazardly pressed more to one side of her head than the other, she was wearing the same clothes she'd had on the day before, and her face was bare of makeup.

His gut constricted.

"So what's up?" he asked her softly, a little alarmed by how easily she allowed him to lead her into the living room, seat her on the sofa and offer her the box of tissues from the end table.

"Nothing, really. I'm...I'm just tired and being stupid."

"And wearing yesterday's clothes."

"Oh!" She glanced down at herself. "I'd forgotten. Sorry." And then, as if becoming aware of her appearance for the first time, she lifted a hand to her hair and then ran it along her wet cheek.

"I'm a mess," she said, obviously embarrassed as she stared down at the carpet.

"You're not a mess," Matt assured her. "I've never met a woman who looked more beautiful *without* all the unnatural help of cosmetics." He could've been saying the words to make her feel better, to be gentlemanly. But he wasn't. He meant them.

She gave him a thoroughly exhausted grin, looking at him from beneath lowered lids. "You don't have to lie, Matt. It's not like we have anything going here."

Seeing her like this, so vulnerable—more vulnerable, somehow, than she'd been that day in the hospital—was doing strange things to Matt's equilibrium.

"It wasn't a lie," he said, sitting down on the edge of the couch, close to her, half facing her. "You wanna tell me what's wrong, or do I start guessing?"

She shook her head. A tear landed on the hands folded in her lap. "You'd never guess."

"I'd guess you haven't been to bed yet."

She wiped her face, then dropped her hand back into her lap. "Actually I have been. Tory called around three this morning. She'd gone into labor and Ben was out of town."

When he heard the explanation, Matt would have relaxed if she hadn't seemed so sad, as well as exhausted. Had something gone wrong?

"Tory was in hard labor for hours and we couldn't reach Ben. The baby was breech and there were some other complications, and they ended up having to do a C-section."

"Is everything okay?"

Phyllis nodded, but the breath she drew in wasn't steady. "She had a little girl—named her after me." She looked up long enough to give him a smile, then looked away again.

Something was wrong. Something had changed her.

"And Tory's okay?"

"Yep. Sore, of course, but Ben's back in town, and mother and baby are both doing fine."

Phyllis was fiddling with the bottom of her sweater, pulling on a thread.

If she didn't stop, she was going to pull the thread all the way through and ruin the sweater.

"You must be exhausted," he said, trying to assimilate the things she'd told him—and whatever she *hadn't* told him.

She nodded, seemingly engrossed with that thread. He suspected she was avoiding his gaze. And he had no idea why. Why had their relationship suddenly become awkward again?

He should probably just leave—let her get some rest. After the night she'd apparently had, she'd be risking the pregnancy for sure if she wasn't really careful. Or maybe...

"Are you bleeding again?"

She shook her head. "No, I'm fine."

He'd like to just believe that and go. Return to his television set. There was still a game and a half remaining, and his Internet friends would be wondering where he was. He hadn't missed a Sunday-afternoon football bonanza in more than two years. They didn't know his real name. Had no idea where he lived or anything personal about him, but they knew ms2456 could call a game like no other.

Something he'd learned from his dad during the times the old man had been around. The elder Sheffield didn't only steal. He also ran a hell of a gambling racket.

"I told Tory about the baby."

He stiffened. "I guess your friends finding out at some point is kind of unavoidable."

She nodded again, the back of her neck looking fragile to him, exposed as it was below her bent head. "I told her to keep quiet about it for now, though. I still want to wait a little while and make sure I'm really going to have this baby before everyone starts making plans for me."

"You're still worried about losing the baby?"

Maybe the night she'd spent, fearing for Tory's baby, had frightened her. Maybe that, coupled with exhaustion, was all that was wrong with her.

"Not really," she said. "No more than I was. But to tell you the truth, I'm enjoying this time alone with the knowledge. It's all settling on me slowly, peacefully, rather than coming at me with hundreds of questions that don't yet have answers."

Matt thought about that, impressed with Phyllis's insight into something she'd never experienced before. "You want time to get some of those questions answered in your own mind before your friends start asking them."

"Yeah," she said. She raised her head, holding his gaze a bit longer before looking down again. "I guess I do."

"I can understand how you feel."

"You're good at that." She sent him a sideways smile.

"Good at what?"

"Understanding."

Hmm. Maybe he was. He'd never thought about it before. He'd just learned at a very young age to put himself in other people's shoes—the people around him—sometimes to predict behavior and get out of the way, sometimes to know when to head for protection somewhere, sometimes to find the love that was never apparent in his house.

Besides, who was he to cast judgment on anyone?

"So you going to tell me what has you so down this afternoon?" he asked. He'd been searching for a way to leave, but suddenly found himself needing to stay. To help her if he could.

"You know—" she looked across at him "—I'd really like to tell you. You're probably the only person who'd understand, but I'm afraid you'll take it wrong, assume I want something that I absolutely do *not* want."

Matt held out both hands, palms up. "I promise, no assumptions."

"This has nothing to do with you."

"Okay."

"You're sure?" She was still watching him. That was good enough for Matt.

"I'm sure."

"Today, when I saw Ben look at that baby..." Tears filled her eyes again and she glanced away, the room in front of her, out the window on the opposite wall, composing herself with obvious effort. "There was such a wealth of love and commitment in his eyes, you just knew that baby was going to be safe for as long as he lived. And beyond, too, because he'll have provided for her."

"And this makes you sad?" Matt wasn't getting it. But he was trying. Were these maybe happy tears?

He didn't think he'd ever seen any, so he couldn't be certain.

"What makes me sad..." She looked back at him, took a deep, shuddering breath. "What makes me so incredibly sad is that my baby isn't going to have that."

His chest constricted. Breathing became difficult. She'd slammed him and he hadn't even seen it coming.

CHAPTER ELEVEN

"YOU SAID YOU WOULDN'T think this was about you."

Her words were so soft it took a couple of seconds for them to register. He was staring at her, but hadn't even been seeing her. Hadn't noticed when her expression had changed from sad to compassionate.

He didn't need her damned pity.

"How can it not be?" he asked more harshly than he'd intended. "I'm the only person on earth who can play that role for your child."

"Biologically, maybe, but I could always marry someone else, someone who'd adopt my baby."

He studied her expression, looking for some sign of insincerity. "You're thinking of getting married?"

What guy was she going to marry? Would he be good to the kid?

"No, I'm not. And that's just it," she continued. "I've had a few relationships, even tried marriage once. I'm much happier alone. I know that about myself. And because of it, my baby's being robbed of something elemental and precious right from the start."

Matt thought about that. What she said made sense. To a point. Especially when you thought about Ben Sanders and the hospital scene Phyllis had just described.

Still...

"Not necessarily," he finally said. His elbows resting on his knees, he clasped his hands together, choosing his words carefully.

"In an ideal world, all children would be born to parents like Ben and Tory Sanders, but that doesn't happen as often as we'd like to think. You, of all people, should know that."

Her face cleared a bit. "You're right, of course."

"The way I figure it, that baby of yours is starting out ahead of the game. He might only have one parent, but she's going to be the best. That kid's going to want for nothing."

She gave a half grin and cocked her head. "You think I'll be a good mother?"

"The best," he said again. He'd have given both legs to have had a mother even half as responsible and capable and obviously caring as Phyllis was. "If I ever chose to have a kid, I couldn't think of anyone who'd make a better mother."

She laughed. "Well, I guess it's a good thing I'm the one you used that faulty condom on, then, huh?"

Her smile took his breath away. Her words hurt more then she'd ever know. And he wasn't even sure why.

Phyllis's face sobered. "You know, Matt, if I ever

chose to have a father for my child, I couldn't imagine anyone I'd want in that position more than you."

No! This had to stop. They were standing at the edge of a deadly precipice. And the wind was blowing. Hard. He could hear it, feel it buffeting his body.

"You have no idea what you're talking about," he said, his voice utterly devoid of warmth. Where he lived, it was rarely warm. And only when he was kidding himself.

She gave him an odd, piercing look. "I do, you know," she said quietly, "although you seem to feel differently."

"I know differently."

"So are you going to tell me why you've decided you're rotten father material?"

It was the soft sincerity of her words that got to him. Made him want things he'd never had.

Made him angry about the wanting.

"The only men in my family I ever knew growing up—my father, my uncle, my older brother—were criminals. Either in jail serving time or out of jail breaking the law."

He stopped, the familiar feeling of shame washing over him, shutting off the words.

Matt stood. It was time to go. Football seemed so far away just then, absurd in its uselessness, yet it called to him. If he could just get home to the game, everything would be normal again—the normal he'd created these past few years.

"What did your brother do?" Her question came as he'd known it would. What he hadn't expected was that she'd remain sitting calmly on the couch. Not threatening him with her presence. Or worse, her touch.

"He raped my baby-sitter."

His words fell harshly into the quiet Sunday-afternoon peace of Phyllis's home.

Shit. Where had they come from? He hadn't thought of that day since it had happened. Hadn't seen his brother since the cops had come to the door and put handcuffs on him, just as they'd done so many times before with their dad.

Brian had been his hero. The one who'd protected him whenever their father was out of jail and came home drunk. He'd never let the old man tease Matt or bully him into doing things Matt didn't want to do.

Like trying to force him to look at the smut magazines all the guys were poring over. Or making fun of his mother or sister when his cruelty made them cry.

He'd cut Brian out of his life that day. Why had he suddenly entered Matt's thoughts again?

"Being related to criminals doesn't make you one."

There was so much noise inside his head Matt was ready to explode. "No?" He turned, pinned her with a harsh glare—reminding himself of his father. "Then perhaps it was my years in jail that did."

He'd never spoken so nastily to another human being in his life. Never allowed himself to be condescendingly cruel as his father had been cruel. It wasn't the words that mattered. It was the way they were said.

Matt had learned that lesson before he'd even learned to talk.

Glancing over his shoulder to catch a glimpse of Phyllis, sitting in the same position, her weary face still wearing kindness, he knew he had to get out of there.

HER HEART WAS POUNDING a little harder than it should from the climb up the stairs to the lighting booth but Sophie decided that was because of the man she was going to see, not the exertion being asked of her body. So what if she was ten pounds under her so-called ideal weight? She was finally starting to look the way she wanted to.

It *had* to be Matt. There couldn't be any other explanation, because she wasn't going to stop losing weight. Not when she felt as great about herself as she did right now. She'd done so well yesterday. A granola bar in the morning to keep her metabolism going. Three-quarters of a cup of dry raisin bran in the afternoon for the fiber, a health bar for vitamins and then a tossed salad, no dressing, at dinnertime so she had her beta carotene. And this morning she'd been down a pound from the day before.

Her size-two pants were a little loose and her waist

tiny enough to draw attention to her breasts. She felt almost good enough to face Matt Sheffield. She had no idea why he liked her so much, why he'd liked her even before she got herself together. And now, well now, she really had something to offer him.

"Hey, Mr. Sheffield," she said as she entered the sound booth. She'd wanted to stand there and watch him work—loved the concentration on his face, the intensity in his eyes when he was creating new illusions with the lights. But she'd been afraid he'd catch her looking and think she was stupid. Or worse yet, young.

He turned just enough to give her a quick smile. "Hey, Sophie," he said.

"You working on the new gobos for the dance show?" She moved over to stand behind him, checking out the images he was manipulating on the computer screen built into the lighting-board table.

Matt jerked kind of nervously when she brushed against his shoulder. "Yeah," he said. "Just let me finish this and I'll be right with you."

"Take your time." She continued to stand there, glad she made him nervous. It showed he cared.

But she'd known that for a while. There were days she felt certain that Matt was the only person in the world who really cared about her.

She didn't mind, though, not as long as she had him. When you had the best, who needed anyone else?

Planning ahead, Sophie went over and sat on the

old green couch. If she stayed by the board, Matt would review the schedule she'd brought him just sitting down at the table. But if she was on the couch, he'd have to join her there. They'd have an excuse to sit close, enjoy each other's body heat, scents. Touch a bit—if only at the shoulders and hips.

She really appreciated that Matt was taking a long time to bring her along, to tutor her in the ways of older men before he made his big move on her. Not that they were all that far apart in age. Only ten years. Hell, of the five husbands her mom had had, four of them were more than ten years older. The fifth one had been eight years younger.

"Almost done," Matt said, his hands moving around the computer keyboard and lighting board with a swiftness and a confidence that Sophie loved.

"No problem," she said, wishing he'd take a little longer. She loved just sitting here in the same room with him.

Couldn't wait until she wouldn't have to use school as an excuse to be close to him.

Taking advantage of the time he'd just given her, Sophie studied Matt, the man who was going to be her next—and last—lover. His hair was black, a little long, and full enough to make her want to run her fingers through it. That was one of the first things she'd do when she finally had the chance to really touch him.

His shoulders were broad, his arms strong enough to easily carry her up those stairs she'd just climbed.

She'd seen him without his shirt once, last year when the electricity had gone out due to a storm and it had been hotter than hell in the theater. They'd had a show that night and shows must always go on, so they'd worked right through the heat, getting sets ready, booms hung and the cyclorama put up. All the technical stuff they could do without electricity.

His chest had been covered with crisp dark hair, his nipples taut on a set of pecs that were rock-solid and beautiful. His back was smooth, the muscles individually delineated, tanned.

Sophie got a little wet just thinking about running her hands along the back she was now staring at, stripping it of the brown corduroy shirt he was wearing tucked into the usual jeans. She continued her fantasy, seeing those shoulders above her, poised over her.

Matt would be a much better lover than Paul. Paul's shoulders were almost boyish, his chest too thin, too bony. Matt's ribs were solid, his abs firm. And his hips—

"Okay, you got the schedule done?"

Sophie blushed when he turned and caught her ogling him, and then, with new confidence gained from her enviably thin body, patted the sofa beside her. "Come and see," she said, smiling with the right amount of innocence and seductiveness—as she'd practiced in the mirror all week.

She couldn't appear too eager, or he might not respect her. Matt was deep; he'd only go for a woman who could meet him on that level. But at the same time, she didn't want to discourage him. She had to let him know that when he was ready to make his move, she wouldn't reject him.

Disappointment crashed through her when he rolled his chair over, still sitting in it, and positioned it in front of the couch. Until she figured out that if she shifted forward, their knees could touch. And their forearms, too, if she held out the schedule at a certain angle.

"I've got Daniel doing preset and teardown," she told him, all business while they discussed the show she was managing that week. "That way, if he does any damage, we'll be the only ones who have to know about it."

"Good thinking." Matt nodded, giving as much attention to her schedule as he had to his lighting design.

This was how she knew Matt liked her so much. He valued every single thing she did.

"What are you going to do with him during the show?" he asked.

"Have him on call in the shop in case of emergency, and toward the end, send him out for pizza and soda. A late supper for the crew before they begin teardown."

"You're good!" Matt gave her the half grin that always melted her insides, his dark eyes meeting hers with such intimacy she almost forgot what she'd been talking about.

They discussed a couple of logistical problems the man on the fly rail was going to need help with during the show—not enough to require a second person but something she'd have to compensate for with someone already on crew. They talked about who'd be doing the lights, who was on audio. She would be calling the show from backstage.

And all the while, Sophie was aware of Matt's knee rubbing almost imperceptibly against hers. Aware of the sprinkling of dark hair on the back of his lean, strong hand.

Aware of those lips, so close to her own.

Someday she was going to make those lips smile. Really smile. Until his eyes reflected the joy he found in her. Thinking about the moment he experienced his first orgasm inside her, with her, Sophie almost couldn't breathe. Her love for him hurt so much.

"...I'd really like you to think about it, Soph."

She'd been watching his lips move, not listening to what he was saying. Figuring it was just more background about the show, she felt pretty confident she could handle that on her own. His abbreviation of her name had been what got her attention.

She loved it when he did that. As if they were intimate enough for him to assume that familiarity. No one called her Soph. She usually forbade it, as the name made her feel gargantuan—and taken for granted. Like an overstuffed piece of furniture. But when Matt said it...

''Think about what?'' she asked when he fell silent, giving her no clue to what he was talking about.

''Speaking with Dr. Langford.''

Sophie stiffened, their future love life temporarily forgotten. ''I don't need a doctor.''

She was on top of things, more aware of her own body, more attuned to taking care of it than she'd ever been before. She knew the dangers of losing too much weight—and she'd watch for them if she ever got down to the weight she needed to be. Until then, she hadn't lost too much.

''She's not a doctor in the medical sense,'' Matt said. His eyes were warm, caring, as he looked at her. It wasn't a look she'd ever seen before. His concern was the nicest gift she'd ever had.

''So what kind of doctor is she?'' she asked, softening. Anything to keep that look focused on her just a little bit longer.

''She teaches psychology here at Montford.''

Sophie frowned, wishing she was a little more clued in. She didn't want to say the wrong thing, sound stupid. Or worse, have him know she hadn't been listening.

It wouldn't matter so much if she could tell him *why* she hadn't been listening. But they weren't that intimate yet.

''I'm a theater major,'' she said, lobbing that one over, hoping it would fly.

''But you had some questions about your future last week....''

"And you cleared them up for me," she assured him quickly. Did he think she wanted to change majors?

God forbid! She couldn't have Matt thinking she wanted to leave him.

"I love it here," she told him, infusing her voice with the love she felt for him.

Matt was such a loner it must hurt him a lot more than most people to be left.

And hurting Matt was the one thing Sophie could never do. She loved him too much.

"I told her a little about you," Matt said. "She thought maybe the two of you could chat, that she could give you some…some womanly insights I wouldn't have. You know, you mentioned about your mother and—"

"You told her about my mother?" Sophie wanted to crawl under the couch and die. Matt had told another woman the things Sophie had shared with him in confidence.

If the humiliation didn't kill her, jealousy would.

"No." She'd been so wrapped up in her own misery, she'd almost missed his reply. Thankfully she didn't.

"I didn't tell her anything specific about what you said," Matt continued slowly. Sophie was particularly fond of the way he chose his words so carefully. So deliberately. It meant he was sincere when he told her how good she was. "I just said that my star student was thinking about quitting school. I couldn't stand by and let that happen.''

"You didn't," Sophie assured him, needing him to know the credit was all his. "You said exactly what I needed to hear. I'm already registered for next semester."

"Good," he said, nodding. He scooted his chair back a little, leaned forward with his elbows on his knees, his hands clasped together between them.

Sophie missed the warmth of his knees. But at least he hadn't ended their meeting.

"I'd still like you to talk to Dr. Langford, Soph," he said when she thought they'd finished with all that. "The doubts might resurface, and I don't want to take any chances on losing you."

Well, when he put it like that... "Then, of course I'll talk to her. Will you set something up for me?"

She really liked the idea of Matt taking care of her this way.

"I'll be seeing her tonight," he said. "I'll speak to her about it then."

Sophie's whole day crashed. He *couldn't* be seeing her tonight. Matt didn't date; everyone knew that. Who was this Dr. Langford, anyway?

She wanted to tell him to forget it, forget setting anything up for her, but then stopped herself. Maybe she needed to meet this Dr. Langford just to set the record straight. Matt and Sophie had an understanding. She needed him. Had been waiting for him to choose the time, day or night, when they'd cross that line from student and teacher to lovers. To the relationship they both wanted so badly.

No psychology professor was going to blow it for them now.

"I can see her tomorrow right before class," she told him, thinking it might be a good idea to have him discuss her with his friend, after all. At least when they were together tonight, he'd be taking Sophie with him.

Dr. Langford couldn't help but get the significance of that.

"I thought you had an English-lit class right before you came to me."

God, she loved it when he talked so possessively. And just that quickly, forgave him for whatever he was doing with Dr. Langford that evening.

"I do, but my teacher's in Phoenix tomorrow giving some paper at ASU. We were allowed to go as extra credit, but I couldn't because it's show week."

She knew he'd appreciate how dedicated she was.

"And you don't want to take advantage of the opportunity to sleep in?"

She about melted right there on the couch when he said that. It made her crazy to know he thought about her in her bed.

"No," she told him. What she wanted was to know, the whole time she was with Dr. Langford, that she'd be going straight to Matt afterward.

"Okay," he said, standing, his hands on the back

of his chair. "Unless you hear from me, plan on being at her office at nine tomorrow morning."

Their meeting was over. Sophie understood. He could only be this close to her for short periods without making a move. He was, after all, a mature and incredibly virile man.

Flicking her blond hair, she smiled at the thought. As for her—she was almost perfect. If he'd only give her another month or two...

CHAPTER TWELVE

"YOU DON'T HAVE to come here at all, but if you're going to come, you can't just take out the trash and pretend that last night didn't happen."

Phyllis had been waiting for Matt to say something the whole ten minutes he'd been in her house taking care of chores. Other than a grunted hello, he hadn't said a word. He was on his way out the kitchen door with the trash and she was afraid he'd just go on home from there.

"I'll be right back," he said, disappeared with the one small bag of garbage he'd collected. He was wearing jeans and a brown corduroy shirt, and from out of nowhere Phyllis was remembering how he'd looked with no shirt at all, those powerful shoulders above her, how the smooth skin, the rippling muscles of his back, had felt to her touch.

She wasn't wearing jeans today. She'd very proudly donned leggings and a long chenille off-white sweater that morning because the button on the black jeans she'd been planning to wear had refused to fasten. A fact she'd bragged about to Tory when she'd spoken with her on the phone after school. Still in Phoenix, Tory was due to come home the next day.

Ben was there, too. He hadn't left the hospital since he'd arrived the day before. Alex was staying with the Montford clan at Montford Mansion.

"Anything else you need done tonight?"

Matt was standing just inside her back door. He was looking at her, but there were no windows to his soul tonight. Only walls.

"I need you to talk to me," she said honestly. She'd been unable to concentrate all day, thoughts of him popping up at odd times, usually when she'd been trying to concentrate on something else.

Like teaching class.

One of her students had reminded her of Matt today. He looked nothing like him. Acted nothing like him. But he'd been wearing a maroon leather jacket...

Moving not an inch from the door, he pulled up the zipper of his brown leather jacket. "I talked to Sophie."

It wasn't what she'd thought he was going to say. "And?"

"She agreed to meet with you."

"Oh!" Phyllis hadn't expected that. At least not so soon, so easily. Maybe the girl wasn't in as much trouble as Phyllis had suspected. "When?"

"Tomorrow morning at nine okay with you?"

"Perfect. That's right in the middle of my office hours."

"Good." He unzipped his jacket, rubbing the tab back and forth between thumb and forefinger. "I might just be wasting your time with her," he said, his free hand on the doorknob. "She seemed fine today. Said she was fine."

Phyllis frowned. "But you told me her lack of concentration's been a problem all semester."

"It has. Today, though, she seemed in top form. We went over the schedule for this week's show and she's done a great job. Had everything well thought out. I couldn't have done better myself."

High praise indeed. She'd have said the words out loud but couldn't rely on his sense of humor. Not at the moment, anyway.

"Could be she ate well yesterday or got enough sleep last night," she said now. "The symptoms you described happened over a period of time. The weight loss, for instance."

"Yeah," he sighed. He rubbed his hand over his face, then pulled open her back door. "I'm sure you're right. I'd really just like the whole thing to disappear."

Phyllis gave him what she hoped was a reassuring smile. "I'll see what I can do."

"Thanks." For a brief moment there was warmth in his eyes. "I'll be in my office if you need to talk to me...."

That sounded very much like goodbye.

Sure enough, Phyllis watched him turn and step one foot outside.

"Wait."

He stopped.

"Matt."

Looking over his shoulder at her, Matt raised a brow in question.

"Can't we talk about last night?"

"I think enough has been said."

She knew that wasn't true. Not by a long shot. But she also knew when to push and when pushing was just going to push someone completely away. Matt was leaving without any push at all.

And if she let him go, he might never come back. Not as her friend. The man she'd slowly been getting to know. The real Matt Sheffield.

So she'd start out slow. See if she could regain the trust she'd done nothing to lose.

"How old were you when you went to prison?"

"Twenty-four." His back still to her, he spoke to her yard.

It was cold outside. She should ask him to shut the door. But the November chill was a small price to find him again.

"How long were you there?"

"Two years."

A long time.

While she did some quick math, he turned around, but his expression wasn't encouraging. She had a feeling he was searching for words that would tactfully tell her to mind her own business.

She had a feeling he wouldn't find any. Because

he *was* her business. If you considered the baby growing inside her.

And Phyllis did. Every minute of every day.

"So you had your teaching degree before you... were incarcerated?"

"My bachelor's. I went for my master's when I got out."

"Did your time in prison have anything to do with your father or your family?"

"No."

"You aren't going to tell me why you were there, are you?"

"No."

"Okay." She nodded, holding his gaze steadfastly. "I can live with that."

He blinked, stared her down.

"I mean it," she said. "You served your time. Whatever you did is in the past. Let's leave it there."

Still he stared. Said nothing.

"The question is," she said slowly, "can *you* leave it there?"

"I left it there the minute I left there."

Arms folded casually, Phyllis crossed one ankle over the other. Retreating with body language. Because it was the only way she *could* retreat.

"If it's behind you, then why should it have any effect on your being a father?"

Clenching his jaw, he stood there staring at her once again, but the invisible barrier between his gaze and hers couldn't be missed. She suspected he was keeping himself in place by sheer force of will. He carefully, deliberately, closed the door.

"The reason I was in prison is not the issue."

"It's not."

"No. I was not guilty of the charges." The words were clipped, succinct.

"But you served the time, anyway."

"Part of it."

Phyllis nodded, consciously slowing herself down. Her thoughts were flying in several different directions. There was so much she wanted to know. She was usually better at waiting people out. Letting them talk in their own time. But with Matt, she had a feeling there wouldn't be such a time. He'd been alone so long that not talking seemed to have become more natural to him than talking.

"So what happened?"

"I was acquitted."

Frowning, she watched him, wishing she could read minds as she'd often been accused of doing. He was confusing her.

"So, if you didn't do anything wrong—and your name's even been cleared—where's the problem?"

"I didn't say I did nothing wrong—only that I wasn't guilty of the crime I was sent up for."

Oh. More questions. Assessing every nuance on his face, she determined that now was not the time to ask them.

"I grew up the child of a convict. My brother grew up the child of a convict. So, for that matter, did a cousin of mine. The stigma that carries does something to a kid.''

''What stigma?''

''Doubt. Fear. People judge.''

Okay, she could see that. ''Why do they have to know?''

''You spend enough time with someone, it eventually comes out.''

She supposed he was right. Holes in one's past were usually revealed, unpleasant truths exposed.

''And they always judge the kid by the father?'' she asked mildly.

''Don't most people judge a book by its cover?''

''Maybe at first, but those who just walk away from it don't matter, and those who pick it up and read it find out almost immediately that a bad cover can hide a gem.''

The muscles in his jaw tightened again. The look in those dark eyes intensified.

''A kid looks to his parents for an example. It's an undeniable and, I think, unchangeable fact. Doesn't matter that the example's rotten, doesn't even matter that the kid *knows* it's rotten, it's still his parent. The person who cares for him, provides for him. The person whose blood runs in his veins.''

She couldn't argue with that. He was absolutely right.

''And when a kid's surrounded by bad examples, he's more apt to believe himself capable of such things.'' His eyes were trained somewhere in the middle of the room, but they were vacant. He spoke in a monotone.

Phyllis stayed perfectly still. Waiting for whatever was to come.

"Even if he determines, because of those examples, to go the opposite way, the values he grew up with are second nature to him. They feel like part of him. Those feelings again guide him to the assumption that he's capable of the bad stuff, too. More capable than someone who grew up in TV-land. And then, one day, bad things start to happen, almost like a self-fulfilling prophecy. Maybe, because he believes he can't help it, he makes a bad choice or two. And once that kid's in any trouble at all, the judging begins. No one's surprised. He is, after all, the son of a convict. His family is rotten. Everyone knows it. They feel sorry for him, but don't doubt his rottenness. They shake their heads and think it's sad the poor kid never had a chance—and maybe wonder how it took him so long to get to this point. And they ask themselves—sometimes loud enough for the kid to hear—what business a man like his father had had fathering children in the first place."

With the help of much practice, Phyllis schooled her face into impassivity, but she cringed inside as Matt's words fell unemotionally between them. Cruel remarks could do so much damage to a psyche. Especially when spoken by adults and overheard by children.

"So what if one of the kid's parents is an ex-con,

but the kid's raised in a home with good values with none of the bad examples?''

Matt blinked, looked at her almost as though he'd just realized she was there. ''The truth will still come out eventually,'' he said. ''And with it, the reputation.'' He'd reconnected with himself. There was emotion in his voice again. Defeat. Resignation.

There was also some truth to his words. Some.

''You're a good man, Matt Sheffield,'' Phyllis said. Her voice might be soft, but it was filled with conviction. ''This isn't the time for you to be a father, we've already decided that, but please don't think you shouldn't ever be one.''

''It's not up for discussion.'' He opened the door again.

''Fine, we won't discuss it,'' Phyllis said, joining him at the door, holding it as he left the house. ''But you'd make a wonderful father, Matt,'' she said behind him.

He stopped cold, didn't turn around.

''You've got the most reliable conscience of anyone I've ever met. What's more, you listen to it. And live by it.''

He stood where he was for a few more seconds and then strode off into the darkness.

He didn't say goodbye.

PHYLLIS WAS READY and waiting for Sophie the next morning. She'd just gotten off the phone with Tory. Her friend was home, up and around, happier than

Phyllis had ever heard her. Apparently Phyllis Christine was the most perfect baby ever to arrive on this earth. Phyllis couldn't wait to go over and see her...see them both.

She'd left the door to her office open and Sophie knocked as she came through. The girl, frighteningly thin, was wearing a pair of stretchy beige hip-huggers and a long gray sweater that showed just how little there was to her stomach and thighs. Her blond hair was fashionably styled but didn't have any luster. Her makeup was impeccable.

She was a beautiful girl.

Sophie sat in the chair at the side of Phyllis's desk. Crossing her legs, a little self-conscious about her own recent weight gain, Phyllis turned her chair so she was facing the girl diagonally.

"I'm glad you could come in." Phyllis tried to meet the girls' eyes, to let her know she meant the words.

Sophie was looking around the room. She shrugged. "Matt asked me to."

Matt? Phyllis was a little surprised, considering how reserved he was, that Matt's relationship with his students seemed so casual.

The girl was still looking around, her eyes not landing anywhere for long.

"You have anything you'd like to talk about?"

Her brows raised, lower lip pouting just a bit, Sophie shook her head. "No. I'm just here because Matt asked me to come."

Yes. She'd already said that.

"Mind if I talk a bit, then?"

Sophie met her gaze for the first time, obviously caught off guard. "No," she said slowly.

"Matt told me you were thinking about quitting school—"

"Only for a minute," Sophie interrupted, her expression earnest. "I'm over that, which is what I tried to tell him yesterday, but he's got himself all concerned, anyway. He's like that, you know."

"Right." Phyllis watched Sophie closely, trying to read between the lines—and through the bravado.

Perusing the room again, Sophie didn't seem able to focus her attention on anything.

Phyllis grabbed a bowl of candy from the cabinet behind her, held it out. "Would you like a piece?" she asked.

"No thanks." Sophie didn't look at the bowl.

Phyllis put it back. She never ate the stuff herself, but liked to have it handy for her students—and the faculty who often stopped by for a dip in the bowl. She enjoyed the camaraderie of their visits.

"Do you like sweets?" she asked.

"Nah." Sophie appeared to be studying Phyllis's degrees hanging on the wall behind her.

"I love them," Phyllis confessed. "Or I did."

Sophie glanced at her and then back toward the degrees.

"I graduated from Boston College," Phyllis said.

"And then Harvard for my masters in psychology and Yale for my doctorate."

"Wow." Sophie sounded genuinely impressed. "You must be smart."

Phyllis shrugged. "Or just good at going to school."

"Yeah, but Harvard *and* Yale?"

"I know." Phyllis rolled her eyes. "Pretty impressive, huh?"

"I'll say."

"Well, I gotta tell you, impressive as those degrees might be, I still ended up doing something pretty stupid with my life."

Sophie stared at her, frowning. "Teaching here? That's not stupid! Montford's one of the best schools in the country."

"No. Not professionally, personally."

"What'd you do?" The girl, leaning back in her chair, skinny legs extended almost straight in front of her, was starting to focus a bit.

"I chose the wrong man to marry, for one."

Sophie's eyes clouded. "Bummer."

"Yeah."

"So you're divorced?"

"Yep."

"How many times?"

An odd question.

"Only once," Phyllis answered, trying not to appear as carefully observant as she was. "I'd had a couple of pretty serious breakups before that, but only one divorce. It's all I intend to have.''

"You say that now."

"I know it," Phyllis assured the girl. "I'm not going down that road again."

"That's what my mom always says."

"Always?"

"Yeah, each time she gets divorced."

"How many times have there been?"

"Five, counting the one she's going through now."

That could certainly cause low self-esteem and emotional insecurity in an adolescent girl.

"What about your father? Do you ever see him?"

"Nah. He left when I was about two. I think he remarried, but my mom never really said for sure."

"You ever consider looking him up?"

Sophie shrugged. "What's the point? He knows where I am if he wants to see me. It's been eighteen years, so I'm guessing he doesn't."

Phyllis's heart went out to the young woman. "You don't know that," she said. "It's possible he thinks you don't want to see him. That he's trying not to interfere in your life."

Sophie looked away. "I wrote to him between husband number three and four," she said with youthful bitterness. "I was just starting high school. He never wrote back."

CHAPTER THIRTEEN

SITTING THERE in her office, facing the chair that had been occupied by numerous students over the past year and a half, Phyllis felt a personal pain she'd never felt with a student before. She wondered if it was because this girl was Matt's star pupil, and Phyllis and Matt's lives were so confusingly tangled at the moment. Or, more likely, she thought, Sophie was just something special all by herself, which was why she'd become Matt's star pupil.

"Maybe your father didn't get the letter."

"He got it," Sophie said dryly. "And even if he didn't, surely he got at least one of the four other letters I sent him before I figured out he really didn't care."

The bastard. That was the type of man who had no business fathering a child. Not someone like Matt Sheffield, who was so aware of the far-reaching responsibilities of fatherhood that he was sparing all future children from suffering because of him.

"Could you have had the wrong address? Maybe he moved."

"He paid child support sporadically—whenever my mom was in between husbands and went after him for it. I got his address off one of the checks she left lying around.''

Warming to the girl, to the problem that wasn't completely unlike her own experience, Phyllis searched for a way to connect—to help Sophie.

''You know, after my husband left, beating me up emotionally on his way out, I had a really hard time realizing that his rejection had nothing to do with me. That the problem was him—not me.''

Sophie looked away, her gaze somewhere around the window behind Phyllis's desk.

''He wasn't home enough to really know me there in the end,'' Phyllis went on, ''but of course, he knew me better than your father knows you. I mean, how can a man who hasn't seen you since you were two even know what he's rejecting?''

Sophie's eyes were bright as she looked back at Phyllis, but although Phyllis waited, Sophie didn't say anything.

''Anyway, after Brad left, I wasn't very smart. I went through a period where I just hated myself. I wasn't woman enough to keep a man. Wasn't pretty enough, sexy enough,'' Phyllis said, telling this special girl something she'd only told her very closest friends. And then, only recently.

''What'd you do?'' Sophie asked quietly, her chin lowered as she watched Phyllis from beneath her lids.

''I punished myself, my body, by eating everything in sight. I was undesirable. I deserved to be fat, to have men look right through me when I walked down the street.''

"But you aren't fat!" Sophie said, her eyes wide.

"Not now. And that leads right into the next stupid thing I did.''

"What?"

Phyllis had the girl's attention now.

"I did a complete reversal. I started punishing myself by not eating at all. For a brief period there, the only time I liked myself was when I went twenty-four hours with less than a thousand calories. And the scariest part was that I didn't know I was still punishing myself. I thought I was finally coming through for *me,* becoming the healthiest, most attractive person I could.''

"Well, it worked," Sophie said. "You look great.''

Coming from someone whose whole life, whose sense of beauty and very sense of self was based on being thin, that was indeed a compliment.

"It didn't work," Phyllis came back immediately. "I realized I wasn't doing myself any good by risking my health. I knew from my research and clinical experience that if I didn't stop, I'd wake up some morning and have to get out of bed in stages because I'd be too dizzy to stand. Or too weak. I'd end up having trouble concentrating. And my emotions would be all over the place.''

Phyllis tried to remember the other symptoms Matt had listed, certain she could name them, too.

Because while she was definitely choosing words that were designed to help Sophie see herself, they were also the truth. Her own lack of perspective on the issue of weight had never been as extreme, or as long-term, but it was something Phyllis had experienced. She understood Sophie's dilemma on a personal, as well as a clinical level.

"Must've been rough," Sophie said. If she was getting the message, she was damned good at hiding the fact.

And to this point, Sophie hadn't been good at hiding anything. Not her nervousness. Or her complete lack of interest in being there when she'd first arrived.

Her genuine fondness for Matt.

"Yeah. The roughest part was recognizing what I was doing. After that, I lost weight the right way. A healthy diet and exercise. It wasn't easy to start eating again, though."

"What's so hard about eating again?" Was that scorn in the girl's voice? Or was Phyllis just so intent on helping Sophie, on helping Matt, that she was looking too hard and seeing things that weren't there?

"When you've learned to hate yourself for every bite you take and love yourself for every bite you don't, having to eat is very difficult. For that first week or so, I'd make myself eat a healthy meal and then feel depressed. I couldn't bear to go out or have anyone see me because I was sure they'd see every single calorie and fat gram as though I were wearing them on top of my clothes, instead of underneath.''

"You could always wear bulky clothes.''

Gotcha, Phyllis thought. Sophie was right there on the journey with her, traveling a familiar road.

"But you have to take them off sometime. To bathe. Change. And what about when you want to go swimming?''

Sophie sat up. "Yeah, well, I'm sure glad I don't have to go through that,'' she said confidently. "I eat too much sometimes, too, but I don't ever gain weight. I guess I'm just lucky to have such a great metabolism.''

As she spoke, Sophie started to flick her right index finger with her thumb. Rapidly enough that Phyllis couldn't help noticing—even if she *hadn't* been keenly observing every nuance of the girl's body language since she'd walked in the door.

Not only was the nail on Sophie's right index finger shorter than all the others, but there was an almost blisterlike scab on her lower knuckle, as well. Phyllis knew what that meant.

She'd bet her life's savings—her baby's college fund—that it wasn't metabolism keeping Sophie skinny when she broke down and went on an eating binge.

"You are lucky,'' she replied calmly, while her mind buzzed with options. "So that's one thing you've got going for you. What are some others?''

If Sophie wasn't ready to admit her problem—it

was entirely possible she hadn't even acknowledged it to herself yet—perhaps Phyllis could take a less obvious path to offer assistance. Eating disorders were usually a physical manifestation of an emotional problem. A symptom. If she could tend to the real problem, help Sophie find value in herself as a person so that she wasn't forced to derive all her worth from her body, then perhaps the anorexia and bulimia would die away.

Sophie had been considering the question quite seriously. Or at least she appeared to be doing so. It was also possible that she couldn't concentrate enough to find an answer at the moment.

Or sadder yet, couldn't find one, period.

"How about your grades?" Phyllis asked. She knew they were good. Matt had told her that. "You ever hit the dean's list?"

"Yeah, every semester since I've been here."

"Okay, that's huge. You know, I have students who have to study nonstop just to get the Cs necessary to stay in this program."

"Bummer."

She wasn't reaching her. Phyllis could feel the girl slipping away.

"So what else would you say you have going for you?" she asked, truly interested. She really liked Sophie, liked the determination she read in the girl's eyes, the ready intelligence.

And she sympathized with the vulnerability she could see just below the surface.

"I'll tell you one thing..." Sophie said, her eyes suddenly alight in a way Phyllis hadn't seen yet. The girl's face took on a whole new beauty, an ethereal, otherworldly aura. And Phyllis had thought her gorgeous before.

"...but only if you promise not to tell anyone." Sophie looked at her intently. "Isn't there some kind of oath or something you guys take that says you can't tell secrets?"

"If I was a practicing psychologist, yes," Phyllis said with an easy smile. Sophie, for all her maturity in some areas, was endearingly young in others. "But you don't have to worry," she said. "The one thing I'm good at is listening to people—helping them—and you can't do that if you hear and then tell." She paused. "The only person I might say anything to is Matt, but only under appropriate circumstances." Phyllis had to be honest about that.

"Well..." Sophie hesitated. With her head lowered again, she looked up at Phyllis, away and then back. Her knee was bobbing. But, as she leaned forward, creating a mood of confidentiality, it stopped.

"You were going to tell me something," Phyllis prompted gently when it appeared that Sophie was having a hard time getting started.

"I have the love of the most amazing man at Montford," the girl said in a rush.

"You do." Phyllis was a little taken aback. Usually eating disorders were a manifestation of feeling unloved.

"Yeah. I've known for a while, but you're the first person I've told."

"And do you love him back?"

"Oh, yeah."

Sophie pushed up the sleeves of her sweater, and Phyllis got a good look at the fuzz on her arms. The girl showed every sign of anorexia. So where was the problem that was prompting the disease? Unless...

"Is he married?"

"Of course not!" Sophie said, sitting back. "I'd never go for a married man. I am *not* going to be like my mom." The girl's knee started to bob again.

They'd come back to that one later.

"So tell me about this man."

Sophie was obviously trying to hold back a smile and then gave up. Lucky man, whoever he was.

"He's gorgeous, for one," she said. "Black hair, taller than I am, slim, but he has all the right muscles in all the right places."

It fit that, obsessed as she was with her own physical appearance, she'd think of the man in terms of looks first. The girl was a case of classic anorexia/ bulimia. Every minute in her company made Phyllis more certain of that.

"He's got hair on his chest, but his back is completely smooth," the girl continued.

So Sophie knew this man intimately, Phyllis concluded, adding this information to the mental list she was compiling.

"My third stepfather had hair all over his back. It was totally gross, like he was some kind of gorilla or something. He used to walk around the house with his shirt off. Ugh." Sophie shivered.

And Phyllis wondered if the man had done anything else to offend the sensibilities of a developing young woman. Another subject they'd return to. If they got the chance.

"So this guy you're in love with is handsome," Phyllis said, guiding Sophie back. If they were going to get anywhere, they had to stay on track, examine the issues one at a time.

"Yeah, but he's far more than that," Sophie said, her eyes soft as a doe's. "He's responsible, reliable. He's smarter than I am, and the greatest artist I've ever known." She glanced at Phyllis, looking a little embarrassed as tears sprang to her eyes. "His talent is amazing to me, Dr. Langford," she said. "There's no end to the images and illusions he can come up with."

Phyllis could relate. She'd thought the very same thing about Matt's talent that day she'd spent with him in the theater.

Of course, with Phyllis, it had just been an appreciation of talent.

"But you know what I love most about him?" Sophie asked, her eyes and voice still full of emotion.

"What?"

"The way he makes me feel about myself. It's like

he thinks I can do anything. And when I'm with him, so do I.''

Phyllis really liked this man. And was suddenly hopeful that helping Sophie wasn't going to be all that difficult. Not when she had a support system like the one she was describing.

''So why haven't you told anyone about him yet?'' Phyllis asked, rocking back in her chair, rolling a pen between her thumbs and forefingers.

''I don't know. I guess because it's still too special.''

''But you're certain he loves you as much as you love him.''

''Oh, yeah. I matter to him. A lot.''

''He's told you so?''

''He tells me all the time, and in ways that really matter, too.'' Sophie sat up straight. ''You should hear him,'' she said, grinning again. ''He's always telling me how much he values me, how much he wants me around. I can't count the times he's told me he doesn't know what he'd do without me. He praises absolutely everything I do, finds good even when it isn't there. You know how love is blind,'' she shared in an aside.

Yes, she did. She'd wasted four years on Brad because she'd been blinded by love.

''And when I'm down or having a problem, he just has to look at me with those dark eyes and there's so much warmth and concern there that it takes my breath away. I only have to be with him for a few minutes and I feel better.''

Phyllis flashed back to the day Matt had taken her to Phoenix. After her exam, while they'd been waiting for Dr. Mac to come talk to them in her office, he'd given her a look similar to the one Sophie had described. Of course, Matt's eyes weren't just dark. They were black.

And while there'd been warmth and concern, the emotions had been impersonal. There'd been no love present.

Still, he'd made her feel better.

"Since he's so eager to be with you, he probably wouldn't be happy that you're keeping him a secret," Phyllis said, homing in on the only thing about Sophie's boyfriend that wasn't making sense.

"He's okay with it," the girl assured her hastily. "As a matter-of-fact, for now, he prefers it that way."

Phyllis's instincts were nagging pretty strongly. There were so many similarities between Sophie's "boyfriend" and Matt Sheffield. Too many?

No. She trusted Matt. If Sophie was telling the truth, she couldn't be talking about Matt.

"Why is that?" she asked. "Why does he want you to keep this a secret?"

"I'm sure it's for my sake," Sophie said, not seeming at all concerned, although both her legs were now bobbing slightly. "He's trying not to rush me, to give me a lot of time so I'm sure about what we're doing. I kind of suspect he wants me to finish school first.''

''You don't know?''

''He's never come right out and said so, but he wouldn't. He wouldn't want to put any conditions on me.''

Hmm.

''Well, I suppose if you're sure you love him, there's no need to rush.''

Sophie's leg-bobbing was becoming more pronounced. ''It's just that...'' She stopped. Phyllis thought she saw a flash of uncertainty cross the girl's face, but it was gone so quickly, confidence once again at the forefront, she couldn't be positive. ''He's older than I am,'' she finished with more than a hint of defensiveness.

The pen between Phyllis's fingers stilled. ''How much older?'' Were the girl's emotions playing a cruel joke on her? Was she trying to find a father and mistaking security for love?

Now *that* could explain the eating disorder.

''Just a little over ten years.''

Not quite father material, then. But within Matt's range.

Stop it, she admonished herself. Matt would never get romantically involved with one of his students. Never.

''And he's uncomfortable about that?''

''I don't think so.'' Sophie shrugged. ''He just wants to make sure I'm with him all the way, doesn't want to rush me through my college years, give me time to sow my wild oats if I need to. I really love him for that. It's just another way he shows me that he's thinking about me, loves me. I've never felt so cared for in my life.''

Phyllis felt increasingly convinced that she wasn't talking about Matt; he would *never* lead a girl on, as this man seemed to be doing. ''And do you need to sow any wild oats?'' she asked mildly.

Think, Phyllis.

''No way. I've always known that when I found the man who was right for me, I'd recognize him—and I'd be done looking.''

Phyllis studied Sophie carefully, her certain expression, the legs now still, her open body posture. ''And you recognize him?''

''Absolutely.''

Or was it just that this young girl had nothing to compare her current lover to?

''Have you had other boyfriends?'' Phyllis asked. She only had about ten more minutes before she had to leave for class. She wasn't finished yet.

''Several,'' Sophie said. ''One of them, Paul, is still hanging around, though I haven't gone out with him since April thirteenth of last year.''

''You remember the day of your last date?'' Kind of remarkable, considering she had no interest in the guy.

''I remember because the very next night he slept with someone else.''

Phyllis filed that information away, too.

"Did you love him before that?"

"I thought I did."

"And how does that feeling compare to what you feel now?"

"There *is* no comparison. The man I love would never be unfaithful. Not ever." One of Sophie's legs was bobbing again. And she was studying her right index finger, frowning as she ran her thumb over the marked knuckle.

Phyllis wasn't quite as satisfied as Sophie that this paragon of virtue was as perfect as he seemed.

If the man loved her so much, was so concerned about her, why didn't he see that she needed help? The symptoms had been obvious even to Matt, and he only saw her a few hours a week in class. During shows and rehearsals, too, but everyone was occupied with work during those intense and busy hours.

Sophie continued to worry her knuckle—and Phyllis continued to watch that slow back-and-forth motion of thumb over forefinger.

The girl was far too confident, considering the very serious problem she had. If Sophie wasn't careful, she was going to kill herself.

"Have you ever made yourself throw up?" Boldness wasn't Phyllis's usual style.

But they were running out of time. If Phyllis couldn't coax Sophie into coming back for another meeting—and since the girl thought she had no problems, getting her to come back wasn't likely—she had to reach her within the next five minutes.

"Hasn't everybody?" Sophie asked, resettling herself in her chair and reaching for her bag on the floor by her feet. "Haven't you ever had too much to drink and known that if you could just throw up, you'd feel better?"

Phyllis had never been much for drinking.

"Have you ever made yourself throw up?" she repeated. "When you think you've had too much to drink—or eat?"

"Sure. Everyone does it."

Yeah, and that's a way to avoid the fact that you have a problem. Convince yourself that "everyone" does it, thus making it normal.

"How *often* does everyone do this?" Phyllis dropped the pen she'd been holding. She had to leave for class now.

And didn't want to go at all.

Sophie slung her bag over one shoulder. "Whenever they have to, I guess." She stood up. "I should get going. I have class in ten minutes."

So did Phyllis. And a hike across campus to get there. She stood, as well, gathered the pile of papers and folders she had ready for her class and left the building with Sophie beside her.

"You mind if we talk again sometime?" the girl asked as Phyllis scrambled for some way to broach the idea of a future meeting without scaring Sophie off.

"Sure," she said immediately; trying to hide her surprise.

Sophie gave a quick shrug. "I think it would make Matt happy if I told him we were going to be friends," she said, stopping as she reached the sidewalk that branched off from the one Phyllis had to take.

Phyllis didn't like the way Sophie had said that. Maybe it was just the fact that she didn't want to be someone's friend just to please someone else. Which, in this case, didn't matter at all. Or was it because Sophie had sounded too possessive of Matt Sheffield?

Phyllis shook her head. She wasn't going to doubt him. She knew Matt. Really knew him.

And he would not—absolutely not—involve himself with any woman, let alone a twenty-year-old student.

For now, Phyllis was just glad she'd have at least one more chance with the girl.

"How about Thursday for lunch?"

Sophie frowned. "I can't then. I've got shows all week."

Phyllis knew that. Matt was going to be working late every night this week. But he was planning to take his dinner hour to drive to her place and do whatever chores needed to be done.

If the bleeding after last Friday's cleaning hadn't scared her so badly, she'd tell him not to come.

"How about Saturday morning, then?" Phyllis asked. She wanted Sophie committed to a time.

"That'd be great," Sophie said, smiling. "Where?"

"The park?" There was only one in Shelter Valley, and it was a popular meeting spot.

"Sure. That's not far from my dorm."

"I'd be happy to swing by and get you."

"That's okay. I'm happy to walk," Sophie said. "I can use the exercise."

As she bade the girl goodbye, Phyllis added that last comment to the list of things she had yet to discuss with her. Was the girl an exercise addict, too? To the point that she couldn't accept a ride to the park? Another symptom typical of anorexics.

Of course, it was also possible that Sophie really did just enjoy a walk now and then.

In any case, the girl had not only agreed to see her again, she'd instigated the meeting.

There was a lift to Phyllis's step as she headed to class. She could help Sophie—and if not, she could get this confused, misguided and oddly appealing girl the help she needed.

CHAPTER FOURTEEN

MATT LOVED HIS JOB. He loved having shows brought to him and making them better. Loved the manipulation, the illusions, the fantasy created by careful staging, painting and lighting.

And the highlight of each day that next week, as he and Sophie and the rest of the students put another show together, was the hour he took away from the theater each evening. Dinner hour.

He'd started going to Phyllis's out of duty. To atone for what he'd done. But he was enjoying himself because of her. Every night that week she'd had dinner waiting for him, insisting that, if he was going to give up his dinner hour to help her, she was at least going to feed him.

And while he stood at her counter and ate, she sat at the table, eating also and talking with him. They covered everything from movies and mountain ranges to the vagaries of teenagers. The part he enjoyed most, though, was just talking about their individual days. It was comforting, somehow, to have someone waiting to hear what had happened in his life that day.

It was something he'd never had before.

And he found himself storing up things throughout the day. He'd have to tell Phyllis that, he'd find himself thinking. And she'd always seem genuinely interested to hear about it later, when he told her.

He also looked forward to sharing *her* day. It almost seemed as if another dimension had been added to his own life. She'd visited Tory each afternoon after school, and Matt really liked the way Phyllis's face lit up when she talked about her friend and the perfect baby Tory had borne. They were calling the little girl Chrissie.

She'd told him about Sophie, too. Matt was surprised to hear about the girl's love interest, able to shed no light whatsoever on the mystery man; he was mostly just relieved that Sophie was talking to Phyllis. And that she was going to do so again. The girl was in good hands. The best.

Thanks to Phyllis, he'd been able to relax around Sophie again as they'd worked together that week. She'd still hung around him a lot, but that didn't worry him so much now that he knew she was leaning on someone else. As usual, he took extra care to praise her for a job well done—because she *did* do a great job—but also because he sensed how badly she needed to know that someone believed in her.

Saturday afternoon, shortly after lunch, Matt showed up at Phyllis's door again. They were planning to take a look at the spare bedroom that weekend to see what they'd have to do to turn it into a nursery.

Phyllis was wearing leggings again—dark gray ones—and a cream-colored knit top that hung halfway down her thighs. She looked beautiful. Far too beautiful.

Matt had been alone for a long time. Why was he suddenly feeling such a strong need for female companionship—and sexual intimacy? Why now?

Considering all the hours he owed Phyllis until she had this baby, his libido couldn't have awakened at a worse time. It wasn't like he had any extra hours to run into Phoenix for a liaison or two.

"How'd it go?" he asked as he climbed the steps to her front porch where she stood waiting for him.

"She was right on time. We had a good talk," Phyllis answered.

"Did you find out who this guy is that she's seeing?"

"No. We really didn't discuss him today, if you don't count the number of times she slipped in a comment about him."

"And the anorexia, did you talk about that?"

"Not really, although I dropped some thinly veiled hints that I thought something was wrong."

They walked into her house. Matt went immediately to the kitchen to get the trash. And then to the laundry room to pick up the basket of clean and folded clothes, ready to go back to the bedroom. He'd carried out the full basket of dirty clothes the night before. And mowed the grass in her backyard the night before that. He'd have done the front, too, she was sure, except that it had desert landscaping.

"So what *did* you talk about?" he asked Phyllis, who was following him as he worked.

"Her stepfathers. I have a feeling one of them did something inappropriate with her."

He turned, frozen. "Raped her?" He could barely get the words out.

Phyllis shook her head. "I don't think it got that far, but he made her feel uncomfortable—and pretty bad about herself."

"Did she tell you that?"

"No, but most of the morning she talked about the third one. He really bothered her the most. She was thirteen when her mother was married to him, and that's a very impressionable age for a girl. It could just be that he was jealous of Sophie. He wouldn't let her mother spend much time with her."

He glanced at her over his shoulder, feeling for the kid. He knew what it felt like not to matter. "You think that happened?"

"I know it did. And the worst of it, of course, was that her mother chose to give in to him rather than put Sophie first."

He understood that, too. Hell, he and the kid had more in common than he'd known. Maybe subconsciously he'd sensed that. And maybe she'd sensed some kind of kindred spirit in him. Maybe that was why they had such a good student-teacher relationship.

Of course, it could also be simply that she was the most gifted student he'd ever had.

After looking at the spare bedroom, Matt decided to take the twin beds down. He was going to store the frames in her garage and the mattresses in an unused room in his house until she decided what she wanted to do with them.

"Any more bleeding?" he asked as he worked on the first bed frame with the wrench she'd provided.

"No."

"When's your next visit?" He was lying on his back, arms underneath the frame as he tried to loosen a bolt from a screw that was stripped. He was certain he had a replacement screw that size in the collection in his garage.

"Monday afternoon. When Dr. Mac released me from the hospital, she said she wanted to see me in two weeks."

"I'll drive you," he said.

"You don't have to do that."

"I'd like to be there."

"Matt…" She'd been sitting on the bed that was still assembled—minus the bedding they'd folded together—but she stood and walked over to the window. "What's going on here?" she asked. "What are we doing?"

Lifting his head enough to see her, Matt quickly returned his attention to the stripped screw. It was an easier battle to face.

"Getting ready to make a nursery."

"That's not what I mean."

He knew that, dammit. "Look," he said, sitting up for a minute, "nothing's changed. We're still working together to get you a healthy baby. The operative word being *you*. As far as I'm concerned, the situation's no different from the first time we talked about this. Except that maybe we've become friends in the process."

She was frowning, looking uncertain, which wasn't usual for her. "You're sure?"

"Absolutely." He was able to stare her right in the eye.

Her shoulders relaxed a bit, but her arms were still wrapped around her middle. "So why go with me to the doctor? It's kind of an intimate thing."

"I'd think sitting with you in the hospital for twelve hours was a lot more intimate than a ride to the doctor's office."

"I guess."

"I just want to be there in case anything comes up," he told her honestly. "You had no idea you were dehydrated the last time you went in, and that landed you in the hospital."

"I've only been sick once all week."

He was very glad to hear that. "Maybe it was only for the first trimester."

"Maybe."

"So you'll let me drive you?"

"I guess," she said, moving back to sit on the

bed. But she didn't seem all that happy about the decision.

Matt wondered why she was having such a big problem with such a small thing.

SHE WAS IN TROUBLE. Wearing another pair of black leggings and a button-down white blouse that reached to midthigh, Phyllis sat beside Matt on the way to Phoenix, telling herself it didn't matter that he was there. That he was no more than a chauffeur to her. Anyone would have done.

And looking over at him—appreciating the fullness of his black hair, the breadth of his shoulders in the black leather jacket, the firmness of his thighs in the black jeans—she knew it wasn't so. That same insidious coiling in her lower belly that had gotten her into this mess was in control again. Leading her to believe she wanted something she didn't want.

Or at least *part* of her didn't want.

The part that had learned life's lessons.

"Do you think there's one special person out there for everyone?" Phyllis asked him.

He glanced over at her and then back at the road. "I think a relationship, any relationship, takes hard work."

She agreed with that. "But given that a person's willing to work hard, do you think there's someone out there for him—or her—to love?"

He was silent for a while and Phyllis pondered her own question. Was it possible that she could fall in love with *someone* who wouldn't feel threatened and defensive when she identified his unstated impulses, his hidden emotions?

"I don't believe there's a certain person for everyone," Matt finally said.

Phyllis's heart sank just a little, but she agreed with him there, too. Running her fingers through her short hair, she determined to recommit herself to the definition she'd come up with for her own life. One that didn't require a man.

Any man.

Including the one by her side.

THE DOCTOR WANTED to do an ultrasound. Phyllis started to panic as soon as she heard, thinking of Matt out in the waiting room, wishing he was in here with her. The bleeding must have been significant, after all. There was something wrong.

"...see if we can get you in today, since you're already in town," Dr. Mac was saying when Phyllis tuned back in.

"Okay," she said, nodding woodenly, bracing herself for what was to come.

"I told you everything's fine," the doctor said, her eyes kind as she sat on the stool beside the examining table.

Scared to death, Phyllis didn't respond. She'd just been through Tory's pregnancy with her and the first eight months of Randi's. The ultrasound didn't come this early in the process unless they were looking for something.

"We've heard your baby's heartbeat," Dr. Mac reminded Phyllis. "It was healthy and strong."

Remembering that miraculous moment only a short time before, Phyllis relaxed. Her baby was alive in there. Everything else they could handle.

She and the baby. Together. Alone. Just the two of them.

"I'm a little curious about how quickly you're showing," the doctor said, still giving Phyllis her complete attention. No writing on charts for Dr. Mac while she was talking to her patients.

It was one of the first things that had impressed Phyllis about the obstetrician.

"Is there some normal explanation for that?" Phyllis asked, nervous again. "Something in particular you're looking for?" Damn. She had to get a grip. This baby had come to mean so much that she'd lost all her normal emotional strength where the pregnancy was concerned.

Dr. Mac shook her head. "I really just want good measurements for the purposes of comparison," she said.

Phyllis could live with that.

AS LONG AS THEY HURRIED, they could get in for the ultrasound before the clinic closed. Phyllis had to drink what seemed like three gallons of water over the course of about half an hour. After that, she was once again leaving Matt reading a magazine in a waiting room while she was led off to another area.

Sitting there in a deserted room full of women's magazines, Matt concentrated on staying calm. He hated doctors' offices. And he hated waiting. He disagreed with all the book reviews in the *People* Magazine he'd found and he thought the celebrity profiles that seemed to appear in every magazine there were trite. And boring.

The colored lights blinking on the Christmas tree set up on a table in the corner were driving him insane. He hated Christmas. All that phony cheer and desperate goodwill. He'd never been part of a real Christmas celebration and probably never would.

You'd think, after thirty-three years, he'd be used to being on the outside looking in. Christmas was the worst time for that.

Damned holiday.

Matt stared at the door through which Phyllis had gone; it was still shut. Though he watched steadily, she didn't come walking through.

Glancing at his watch, he saw she'd only been gone about twenty minutes.

How long did ultrasounds take?

She'd said the doctor only wanted measurements. Matt continued to watch the door. If anything happened to that baby...

For Phyllis's sake, he put every ounce of mental energy he possessed on the other side of that door, in whatever room they were doing the ultrasound. That baby had to be fine. Phyllis needed it so badly.

And there was no one who deserved it more. Phyllis was the greatest woman he'd ever met. He'd never known anyone who just kept giving and giving the way she did. There seemed no end to the fount of her caring for those around her. Here she was, lying low, having a tough time of it, handling things all alone—and helping Tory birth a baby, helping to save Sophie from herself. And saving Matt from himself, too.

Dropping the *People* magazine back to the table, he stood, fingertips in the front pockets of his jeans. Where on earth had that last thought come from? He didn't need saving.

He'd saved himself years ago. Had a life now. A good life.

His heart jumped when the door opened, and he waited to see who came through.

It was Phyllis. And she didn't look right.

"All ready?" he asked, trying to assess the seriousness of the situation by her expression. And failing completely.

"Yeah," she said, nodding. Her eyes, when she smiled at him, were vacant. As vacant as the smile itself.

"You need to see anyone about paying?" he asked as she walked, very subdued, toward the door.

"No." She shook her head. "They have my insurance information."

Matt held the door for her, following her into the sunshine. She walked silently to the car, her face blank, slid in and buckled her seat belt.

And then she sat, staring straight ahead, with apparently no interest in where they went next.

Matt was afraid to ask what she'd just found out. But he had to know how bad it was. Had to know if it was fixable.

"It's after six. You want some dinner?" he asked, buying himself time.

"Okay."

Other than that day in Tortilla Flat, a day that seemed so long ago now, they'd never actually sat at a table together to share a meal. But he knew exactly what she'd like.

Phyllis loved pasta. Of any kind. He drove to the Macaroni Grill.

But once he'd parked in the lot, he couldn't go in. Not until she talked to him.

"So how bad is it?" He could have phrased that question a whole lot better if he hadn't been just about ready to explode with tension. The silent drive from the doctor's office had been the longest ten minutes he could remember in years.

Phyllis started, looked over at him. It took her a second, but her soft green eyes finally focused. "How bad is what?" she asked, gazing around. The place was decorated for Christmas. "The food here? It's good. Really good. Haven't you eaten here before?"

She released the buckle on her seat belt.

"Yes, I've eaten here before," he said, studying her closely.

"So," she said, turning to him again when he made no move to leave the car. "We going in?"

"As soon as you tell me what happened back there."

She sighed. Looked a little scared. And then gave him a shaky smile. "There were two of them."

He frowned. "Two of what?"

"Babies."

She'd lost him completely. "Where?" There'd been no one in the waiting room when they'd come in. He'd assumed they were the only people at the clinic.

"Here," she said, patting her belly.

Oh.

Oh.

Matt felt the blood drain from his face. Curses strung themselves together in his mind.

"Two," he said in a questioning tone—almost as though, if he gave her another chance, she'd change her mind.

"Mmm-hmm."

Damn.

He still wasn't sure he could ever atone for *one*. How in hell would he make up for two?

For deserting two?

Shaking his head, Matt lowered his hands, keys clutched in one fist, to his lap. That last thought had snuck up on him. Caught him unawares. He was deserting his own child. *Children.*

He, *they,* were going to grow up knowing their father hadn't wanted them.

How could he do that to him? To *them?*

And yet, considering his own childhood, the judgments passed on him because of his father's sins, how could he not?

"Matt?"

He turned to find Phyllis looking at him, her eyes completely lucid now and filled with concern.

"It's okay."

"What's okay?"

"The fact that there are two babies, instead of one. It doesn't change anything. It doesn't have to affect you at all."

"It means I'm twice as responsible."

"No!"

"Yes."

"I'm not going to have you beating yourself up over this," she insisted.

But she was too late.

CHAPTER FIFTEEN

TWINS. TWICE THE WORK. Twice the bills. Twice the diapers and bottles and cribs. Twice the high chairs, the pacifiers, the clothes. Twice the love.

And twice the amount of time she was seeing Matt, too. Phyllis was going through the box of Christmas decorations Matt had lifted down for her from the shelf in her garage. He was taking her to get a tree, and because she knew him well enough to know he'd insist on stringing the lights for her when they got back, she wanted everything ready.

She felt really guilty for taking up so much of his time—even more of it, now that he knew there were two babies ''to make up for,'' as he put it.

As if he needed to make up for them at all!

She wished he could see that he'd given her the greatest gift she'd ever had.

It had only been two days since the ultrasound, and he'd already painted the nursery. At this rate, he could have an entirely new house built for these children before they ever put in an appearance.

She was ready and waiting, wearing black jeans with a maternity panel—borrowed from Tory—and a thick cream-colored sweater when Matt came to the door. She told him about her most recent meeting with Sophie as they drove outside town to the lot where everyone had told her to get her tree.

"She's planning to stay in Shelter Valley for Christmas," Phyllis said. "I guess her mother mentioned a new boyfriend who's going to be spending the holiday at their house, and Sophie can't bear the thought of being around for the wooing process of husband number six."

"Yeah," Matt said, driving slowly through town. "She told me the same thing. Poor kid."

"I guess there's one dorm that's kept open during the break, and everyone who's staying on campus moves there for those weeks."

Matt nodded. "I've heard about that. They do a gift exchange and cater a Christmas dinner for them."

"Apparently there are some pretty wild parties, too." Or at least Sophie wanted her to believe there were.

"I hadn't heard about those."

His eyes on the road, Matt drove steadily, but he didn't seem to feel very involved in their outing. Phyllis wondered why. She began to worry that all this service he'd been providing was getting to him, wearing thin.

All the more reason to do something for him.

"I was wondering...," she said slowly, and then stopped, reconsidering what she'd been about to ask.

"What?" He glanced over at her, and the warmth

in those black eyes, visible in the shine of the dash lights, had her up and running again.

"Well, I just thought that since I'm alone and you're alone, we could have Christmas dinner together and—"

Matt shook his head before she could even get the question completely out. "You don't have to do that," he said.

"I want to."

"It's not necessary, Phyllis," he said. "I'm sure half a dozen of your friends have invited you over for their family celebrations."

"Most everyone's going to be at Becca and Will's," she said.

"Then you should join them."

He was right. She probably should, but... "I don't want to join them."

"Isn't that what you did last year?"

"Yes."

"Well, don't change things on my account."

Maybe they were already changed. Without her having any say in the matter. "Other than Tory and Cassie, they still don't know about the baby—*babies,*" she confessed.

"Do Tory and Cassie know you're having twins?"

"Tory does. Cassie's been in Connecticut this past week doing a symposium on pet therapy."

"How much longer do you think you need to wait before you tell the others?"

Phyllis shrugged, her arms wrapped around her stomach. "I don't know," she told him honestly. "I'm just not up to all the questions right now. All their concern. I know they're going to make me feel so helpless, falling all over themselves to look after me because I'm single."

"And that's bad? To have friends who care for you that much?"

"Of course not! I just don't want their pity."

Silence fell as they turned away from town and headed out to the tree lot. Matt had worked until after dinnertime that night, and it was already dark. Phyllis watched for the occasional Christmas-tree lights glittering on homes in the distance.

"I really want to make my own Christmas dinner." She broached the subject again, in spite of the fact that she figured she should leave well enough alone. If Matt wanted to spend Christmas by himself, who was she to interfere?

Just the woman who loved him...

No! Phyllis jerked her head away from him. She felt an absurd, superstitious fear that if he could see her face, the thought she'd just had would somehow reveal itself to him. She stared out the side window.

"So make it."

His reply confused her, until she remembered what she'd just said. And why she'd said it.

The reason was still valid. The plan was a good one.

And she was strong enough to put her own insecurities aside to support a friend.

"I'll need help," she said, only a little ashamed at playing her ace. Was she so desperate for his company that she'd actually manipulate him to get it?

God, she hoped not.

The plan was to make sure he didn't spend the holiday alone. To show him he *wasn't* alone.

That he had a friend in the world.

"Help how?" he asked.

"Lifting the turkey in and out of the oven for one." That would keep him there for a good part of the day while the bird cooked. "Carrying the pot of water to the stove for the potatoes."

Okay, she was digging a little deep on that one.

He nodded. His chin was jutting out, his thumb tapping on the steering wheel.

"You're doing this on purpose, aren't you," he said, his eyes never straying from the road.

"Probably."

"It's that important to you?"

"Yeah."

"Then let's do it."

"You're sure?"

He hesitated, but only for a moment. "I'm sure."

Phyllis bit her lip. "And would you mind terribly if Sophie joined us? Just for dinner, not for the day," she added hastily. "I hate the thought of her being there in a dorm with strangers."

"No, I don't mind." He finally glanced her way,

and his eyes, at least in the dim lights, appeared to be filled with warmth. "As a matter-of-fact, I think it's a nice idea."

Phew. All in all, that had been easier than she'd expected.

HE'D NEVER BOUGHT a Christmas tree before. Not completely clear about the process, Matt was happy to assume his role of assistant, on hand to do the heavy work and simply trail around after Phyllis. He pulled up the collar of his jacket against the evening chill as he locked the Blazer.

The tree lot, set up out in the desert, occupied more than an acre.

"Where do you want to start?" Phyllis asked him, walking across the straw scattered all over the ground, shuffling her feet like a little kid. She was grinning.

"Wherever you'd like."

In the center of the lot was a bonfire, with several people—mostly women and children—huddled around it.

"I got a Fraser last year and really liked it. What do you think?"

A Fraser? Matt had a feeling they weren't talking about television shows.

"Sure."

"I want a tall one." She turned in a circle, surveying the lot. "I can't tell how they're arranged here."

At a complete loss, Matt looked around for someone who worked there. He saw several college-age guys wearing sweatshirts, dirty jeans and gloves, but they were all helping other people. The lot was doing a booming business.

"I guess you should just pick a tree you like and we'll go from there," Matt said.

"Which ones do you like?"

"How about this one?" he asked, stopping by a fir that was tall and green, had a classic Christmas-tree shape and was full enough that he couldn't see the base.

"It's a Douglas."

Was that a good thing?

"Douglases don't live as long as Frasers or Nobles. Their branches start to droop almost immediately, and they lose their needles the quickest." She frowned, considering the tree. "They are the cheapest, though, and the most beautiful."

"But if they don't last, what does beauty matter?"

Phyllis's eyes were serious as she looked up at him. "It's only six days until Christmas. I'm sure it'll last that long."

Still, she continued walking, checking out—or so it seemed to Matt—every single tree on the lot.

"Do you think I should get a Noble?" Phyllis asked, stopping by one of the sorrier trees he'd seen. "The branches are sparser, but the needles are soft and Nobles live the longest."

"But if you can't stand the sight of it..."

Phyllis gave him a startled look over her shoulder and then grinned. "I guess you're right. They're the most expensive, anyway."

A couple of kids pushed by them, running to show their parents the tree they'd picked out. "This one!" they were hollering. They seemed to be having a great time.

Watching those kids, Matt couldn't relate. Couldn't relate to how it felt to be a kid picking out a tree, anticipating the packages that would soon lie underneath it.

"What about the Frasers you were talking about?" Matt asked Phyllis in an effort to move her along.

They found several Frasers that were over seven feet tall, just what she wanted. And still the job wasn't done. Phyllis walked around each tree, examining it carefully. You'd think she was buying a piece of furniture that was going to last her until the next century, not a tree she'd be throwing out in a little more than a week.

"I like the shape of this one best," she said slowly, circling a tree. "But it's got this bald spot."

Matt went to see. She was right.

"And this one looks good all the way around, but the needles are already brown on the base and on the ends of those branches."

Didn't sound good.

"What do you think?" She turned toward him,

acting as though the tree meant something to him, too.

It didn't. Not any more than those babies she was carrying.

Babies. Two of them. For a moment there, he'd actually forgotten. How in hell could he walk away and leave her to fend for herself with *two* babies?

"I think it's a toss-up," he told her when he realized she was waiting for him to answer.

"Why don't you get one and I'll get the other?"

"I'm not getting one."

Phyllis left the tree, walking back to him, a puzzled expression on her face. Her nose was turning red from the chill in the air. She looked young and cute and far too beautiful.

"You already got yours?" she asked. "I'm sorry to have to drag you out a second time. I thought you had to come, anyway."

"I don't have one." Fingers in the pockets of his jeans, Matt hunched his shoulders against the chill, facing the two trees. "I'm not getting one," he said again.

And she'd better get hers quickly. He'd been there long enough.

"Why not?"

He shrugged.

"Don't you believe in Christmas?"

"Sure. I guess." For other people. Any religious beliefs he did or didn't hold had nothing to do with a day that had no relevance to an event that took place more than two thousand years before. December twenty-fifth was just a day. A day that had as much to do with pagan festivals as Christian ones.

"You never buy a tree?"

"No."

"Not ever?"

"No."

She was standing beside him, and he could feel her looking at him, could tell from the direction of her voice that her face was turned toward him. He wondered if there was another tree close by that was perfect, waiting for her to buy it and get it out of there.

"When's the last time you had a tree?"

Matt clamped his jaws shut. It was either that or say something he'd have to feel bad about.

"Never," he said when he had his tension under sufficient control and could at least sound civil.

"I don't mean since you've been on your own," she said, moving so close to him that their arms touched as she adjusted her footing on the straw. "I mean ever."

"I've never had a tree. Or presents, either."

A family—mom, dad and three kids—came close enough to be within earshot. They were looking at one of the two trees Phyllis had been considering. She stood there in silence, apparently unconcerned that she was about to lose her Christmas tree, until they'd decided the tree was too expensive and moved on.

''Not even as a kid?'' she asked softly as soon as the family was out of earshot.

''Nope.''

Her hand sliding into his shocked him into complete stillness. Not only because they didn't touch. Ever. But because there was a completely unfamiliar comfort in having it there.

''I'm sorry.''

Had the words been filled with pity, Matt would have been able to disregard them. But they spoke of caring, of empathy, of genuine sorrow at a perceived injustice, and he could do nothing for a moment but stand there, her hand in his, and swallow the emotion that had risen to his throat.

THAT NIGHT Phyllis broke her own rules. She knew there was no place in her life for a man, that to stay emotionally healthy she had to keep her heart guarded. And to do that, she had to keep an emotional distance—and if necessary a physical one—from any man she started to like too much.

The plan worked. She had a couple of happy years behind her to attest to that.

But Matt Sheffield needed her. So she was going to be there for him. It was no wonder the man had no faith in himself, in the magic of unconditional love, of giving *and* receiving. He'd never had Christmas.

And the absence of Christmas—in his childhood,

especially—was symbolic of so many other absences, other deprivations....

She had to change that.

"Could you put these near the top?" she asked, handing him four little glass angels that Christine had given her a few years before. She'd said they were because Phyllis was her own private angel.

Yet Christine had been the angel among them. And now, the angel watching over them?

Matt placed the angels wordlessly, just as he'd wrapped the lights around the tree and helped her with the unpacking of other ornaments. She'd tried to share their significance with him, but after the first couple she'd stopped. The stories seemed more painful to him than anything else. He didn't even seem to see the work they were doing. The beauty they were creating.

He was helping her, but he wasn't there with her.

"If you don't need anything else..." His words faded as he looked around. She had several boxes of ornaments left to hang, but the top of the tree was full. It was obvious she could do the rest with little effort.

"Actually, I need you to wait for a while if you could," she said.

He seemed surprised by the unusual request—and maybe a touch resentful—but then capitulated. "Of course."

"It's because the star that goes on the very top of

the tree has to be the last thing up, and I'm going to need your help with it."

"Fine." He wasn't looking at the tree. He surveyed the boxes she had yet to get through, his expression vacant.

"And since you've done so much of the work, you have to have some hot chocolate, too."

"I don't need any hot chocolate."

"Yes, you do, Matt, trust me," Phyllis told him. "You just don't know it yet." They were making a Christmas memory for him here—a little piece of magic he could carry with him all year round to remind him that there was life and beauty and spirit beyond the ordinary. And Christmas memories had to include at least one cup of hot chocolate.

"Then how about I go in and make the hot chocolate while you finish up in here?" he suggested, the words more statement than question.

It wasn't quite the scenario Phyllis had in mind. He was supposed to be decorating his first tree. But having him actively engaged in the kitchen was a whole lot better than not engaged at all.

"Great," she said, determining to do the fastest decorating job in history. "The pan's in the—"

"I know where everything is."

The intimacy of that statement made Phyllis smile inside.

But the smile faded when he strode quickly from the room, making it obvious that he couldn't get away fast enough.

She loved Christmas. Cherished hours she spent decorating her tree. Because with every decoration there was a memory of love given or received. Each one brought a remembrance of a particular loved one.

For her, Christmas was the epitome of all that was good in the world.

And Matt had never experienced a Christmas moment in his life.

He was a man so complete unto himself that there was no door by which anyone could crash his private party.

Phyllis had to wonder if she'd set herself an impossible task. Perhaps there really was no way to remove those shadows from Matt's eyes. From his heart.

By the time she placed the last ornaments on the tree, tears were dripping slowly down her face.

CHAPTER SIXTEEN

HE HAD TO GET OUT of there. Much more of Phyllis's Christmas and he was going to lose his perspective.

"This is great!" she said, sipping the cup of chocolate he'd poured for her. She was sitting in her usual seat at the end of the kitchen table while he stood in his usual spot by the counter.

"So we just have to put on the star and the tree's done?"

A minute or two more, and he could make his escape back to the things he knew, the life he understood.

When she didn't answer him, Matt looked up from the geometric design in the tile he'd been studying. The tears gathering in her green eyes brought dread to his gut. And a tightness to his chest that he hadn't felt in a long, long time.

She was going to ask something of him that he couldn't give. The walls were closing in.

Matt thought longingly of his Blazer in the drive. And the deserted expanse of open road just outside town.

"Please tell me why you were sent to prison."

Matt blinked, took a moment to switch gears. He'd

been expecting a question about his childhood. Or a challenge regarding his future.

And actually found the topic she'd chosen preferable to either of the other two. At the moment it would be the easiest one to address.

And maybe the answer would put a stop to whatever was happening here that he didn't understand. It would certainly establish very clearly—for both of them—that he was not the man to be a father to those babies. It would reerect the barriers between them, barriers that had slipped without his noticing it.

"Please?" Her question was barely a whisper.

Setting down his cup, Matt leaned back against the counter, crossing his ankles, bracing his hands on either side of him.

"I was twenty-four, teaching junior-high- and high-school theater," he started, his gaze directed toward her but seeing inward.

He couldn't do this if she was going to keep looking at him as if he really mattered.

"Your first job?"

And not if she intended to take this journey with him. He needed her to be a silent listener, not a participant.

"Yeah. I was in my second year, though."

"Where?"

"Flagstaff."

"Where you grew up."

"Yeah." And that mistake had been one of many.

"I had some crazy idea that I'd go back and show them all that I'd made something of myself."

"And help some of the other kids who were having as hard a life as you'd had?" she asked, her elbow on the table, chin resting in her palm.

Matt studied her with an intensity he couldn't hide. He'd never told anyone that. Was rather ashamed of what an idealistic fool he'd been back then.

"I'm sorry," she said, her eyes warm as she continued to watch him. "I'm way off base, right?"

"No," he heard himself admit to her. "But how did you know that?"

Phyllis shrugged. "I know you."

"Yeah?"

"That's the type of man you are, Matt, always thinking of the other guy, giving every ounce of yourself to someone else, never to yourself."

He wanted to deny her words for the nonsense they were, but he couldn't speak for a second or two. It was long enough for her faith in him to fill up places he hadn't known were empty.

Shaking her head, Phyllis let her hands drop to her lap, slide together between her knees, as though she were putting them under lock and key. "I'm really sorry, Matt," she said. "I have a tendency to do that—to work out other people's feelings and motivations."

"No, don't apologize," he said, finding his voice. "Whether it's true or not, I like what you see."

Of course, her perception of him was about to change...

"There was this girl in a couple of my classes, involved in the community theater where I volunteered—and then she signed up for drama at school, helping me with sets and lighting for the annual school production. Her name was Shelley Monroe."

It was still her name—the one Matt wrote on a check every single month. She'd wanted more from him, wanted them to write to each other, keep open some form of communication. Matt had refused.

But he never missed a month sending her those checks. They were all he could do for her.

He thought back over the months with Shelley, trying, as usual, to see in them something he'd missed, something that would change what came after. And, as usual, failing.

"Tell me about her."

"Shelley was very troubled and old beyond her years, but an extremely promising student. Her home life was hell, an alcoholic father, an abused mother—you can imagine..."

Phyllis nodded, her eyes knowing.

"Yet, in spite of seeing things a kid her age should never see, Shelley was a great kid, smart, ambitious, reliable. She worked her ass off, doing whatever job she was given."

"Kind of like Sophie."

Matt hadn't made that connection. "Maybe," he

allowed, considering the idea. "In some ways." And in other ways not at all. But that was yet to come.

"I could relate to her," he continued. "And I was a living example that you could come from a home like that and still make something of yourself. If you had what it took and were willing to put every bit of your soul into trying.

"Shelley had what it takes, and I was determined to *make* her succeed. I spent a lot of time with her, demanding that she give her best, encouraging her to use her talents, stretch them, convincing her she could make something grand out of less-than-stellar beginnings."

Matt swallowed. Wished he had a shot of whiskey. Or at the very least a cold beer.

"That was, after all, the reason you were there. Teaching."

Yeah, he supposed it was. So why hadn't anyone else ever seen that? Of course, by the time anyone else was involved, things had already gotten too far out of hand.

Staring at the back door, Matt went on, his tone as emotionless as the rest of him. The past...well, it was what it was. There was nothing he could do about it.

"I made a point of telling her often how much value I saw in her. As is the case with most kids in her situation, she was pretty low on self-esteem. She really believed that because of what she'd seen and done, there was no innocence left in her, no goodness, and that no decent man was ever going to want to marry her. And my comeback—because I couldn't let statements like that go—would always be to tell her that when she was older, any man would be lucky to have her as his wife."

A quick glance in Phyllis's direction showed him how completely still she was. Just as she'd seen his reasons for taking that damn teaching job in the first place, she'd probably jumped ahead in this story, too.

His gaze back on the door, he continued, "While I was busy trying to build her self-esteem, she was misinterpreting my interest. One Saturday we were at school working on a particularly complicated set design when she suddenly didn't feel well. She was sweating, white as a sheet and her vision was blurred. One side of her head hurt intensely. I recognized the signs of a migraine—something she'd suffered from before—and offered her an analgesic and the use of my office couch until she felt better."

"You never give a student medicine."

"I know."

"I'd have done the same thing."

His eyes met hers, locked on.

"She slept for a long time and when I finally tried to rouse her, it wasn't easy. She was groggy for a while, but eventually got up and went home."

Matt paused, having difficulty proceeding any further. Phyllis didn't help him out as she had before.

"A month later she was pregnant," he said, avoiding Phyllis's side of the room completely. He didn't want to see if the expression in her eyes had changed. "She named me as the father."

"But you never touched the girl!"

He glanced quickly over at her and away. She was still with him. His breathing came a little easier.

"She believes we slept together that day in my office."

"But surely you could prove…"

Matt shook his head. "What could I prove? The things I was saying to her could've been misinterpreted to mean that there was more between us than I intended."

"You were an adult. She was a child."

Matt sent her a stare that brooked no argument. "Which is why, when the jury heard her testimony of the things I'd been saying to her, they sent me to prison."

"It didn't matter that you told them you'd never thought of her in those terms?"

Matt took a deep breath, his brows creased as he brooded over the honest answer to that question. Holding her gaze, he said, "I never for one second crossed the line to inappropriate feelings for a fourteen-year-old child. But in all honesty, I was maybe falling a bit in love with the woman I knew she could become someday."

The kitchen was completely silent.

When Phyllis finally moved, it was to put her cup

in the sink, grab his hand and tug gently. "Let's go into the other room," she said.

Though he had no idea why, Matt blindly went.

When they got to the living room, she turned off all but the Christmas-tree lights. They gave the warmest glow he'd ever seen. Almost like firelight with comforting flashes of color. A strange serenity spread through him as she pulled him over to the sofa with her and sat.

The woman was some kind of sorceress.

One Matt could easily become addicted to.

"I led her on." His voice was hushed.

"Not intentionally. And not at all if she'd been rational. You can't be blamed for her irrationality."

"Yeah, try taking that to court."

"Tell me the rest."

He leaned into the couch, one ankle crossed over his knee and stared at the lights. "It was her word against mine. She claims she remembers waking up in my office a couple of times, remembers me sitting there, holding her shoulders, talking softly to her."

"You were trying to wake her."

"And at one point to get her to sit up."

Again he went back to that day. And it was always the same. "Hindsight says I should've called someone in to sit with us. Hell," he said harshly, "hindsight says I should've played the entire thing differently."

"What, left her to rot in the hell that was her life?"

"Being pregnant at fourteen is a better alternative?"

"But you didn't make her pregnant."

Maybe not, but...

"If I hadn't encouraged her to see herself as a desirable woman, chances are good she wouldn't have turned to sex for the love and acceptance she needed."

"But you didn't know that."

"And that's the point. I had no business getting involved with her. I should've been the best damn teacher I knew how to be—and sent her to a counselor for the rest of it."

"You were twenty-four years old, Matt."

"Old enough to be accountable, as the jury quickly decided." He paused, rubbed his hands on his thighs. "The best I can tell, Shelley must have dreamed that she and I slept together that day and then somehow the dream got mixed up with the bits of reality she remembers. Next thing I knew, I was being sent up for ten years to pay for a crime I only partially committed."

Phyllis placed her hand on his. "You didn't commit any crime at all. You *cared.* And in any book that counts, that will *never* be a crime. I can't speak for the justice system, Matt, but any real judging is a judging of the heart, of intention and motivation."

He looked into her eyes, so close to his own, and felt a soothing of the pain that had been festering inside him for six long years.

He wanted to kiss her. Needed to kiss her.

"So what happened?" she asked, bringing him gently back to earth, reminding him that kissing wasn't what they were about.

"When the baby was six months old, old enough for a conclusive paternity test, it was proved that I wasn't the father."

Phyllis nodded. He knew he should look away. Had to look away. But not yet. The warmth surrounding him was so new, so foreign, so compelling that he couldn't deny himself just yet.

"The case went back to trial…"

"I'm surprised that was even necessary with such conclusive proof."

"Technically I wasn't in prison for impregnating Shelley. I was doing time for statutory rape, and just because Shelley had been with someone else didn't mean she hadn't also been with me."

"But obviously that was proved, as well."

Matt shook his head. "Not really. Not completely. But because the first time around, Shelley had sworn that she *hadn't* been with anyone else, my attorney was able to discredit her testimony enough to put doubt in the jurors' minds. Because of that doubt, I was set free."

"And since you weren't conclusively cleared of guilt, you could no longer do your job in that district."

"Or in the entire city, or probably in any other

public-school system. Something like that marks a man.''

''In more ways than one.''

Matt frowned. ''What do you mean?''

''It marked you publicly, but the marks it made inside you are even worse, aren't they?''

He didn't say anything, wasn't at all comfortable with her insights. And yet... A couple of times now she'd been able to take his experiences and turn them around, reveal a whole new aspect, so they no longer resembled the burden he'd been carrying. She'd bought him some freedom. Still...

''I hold myself accountable for my actions,'' he said stubbornly.

''And your actions show very clearly that you're a good man who, out of youth and idealism, made a couple of calls that weren't the best. But they're calls you've never made again. There've been no repeat performances in all these years.''

He'd made damn sure there weren't.

And maybe that was exactly what she was talking about. He was so used to seeing himself as the man who'd made those bad calls that maybe he'd been blind to the man he'd become. And yet, he remained accountable for those bad calls. Was still paying the price. Both metaphorically and literally.

''I think Shelley really believes we had sex that day.''

''Because she needs to, maybe.''

''What do you mean?''

"Think about it, Matt. If someone like *you* wanted her, she'd feel a whole lot better about herself than if it was just some scum on the street, some guy who'd sleep with a fourteen-year-old."

He considered the idea. And released a heavy sigh as something else finally fell into place for him.

"You know," he said, "all these years I've never been able to understand something that suddenly makes perfect sense."

"What's that?"

"When all this first started I asked Shelley why, if she cared about me so much, she'd do this to me, get me into so much trouble, when all I was trying to do was help her.

"She said because more than she needed me, she needed a father for her baby."

"And whoever the other guy was, he wasn't father material," Phyllis added. "Even in prison, you were father material."

And out of it, too, according to Shelley. But at least now he understood. The kid hadn't turned her back on all he'd done for her. She'd just been desperate to take care of herself. It changed nothing; the facts were still the facts. And yet, in some way, everything had changed.

When Matt looked for the self-loathing that was as much a part of him as his heart and lungs, he couldn't find it.

Phyllis leaned over, bringing her mouth slowly, tenderly, to his.

The woman was a miracle worker. A sorceress, just as he'd thought.

IT WAS THURSDAY after work.

He was going to be there any minute.

Phyllis commanded herself to concentrate on the paper she was grading—one of about twenty term papers she had to get through before the following afternoon—the last day of school before the winter break.

Her job was the important thing.

Not Matt Sheffield, biological father of her kids and temporary handyman.

No matter what a great guy he was, what a terrific human being, what a spectacular kisser, no matter how much it had meant having him there while she decorated her tree, he wasn't important to her.

He *couldn't* be.

The phone on her desk in the corner of her living room rang, and Phyllis stared at it, thinking about picking it up. It could be Matt saying he wasn't coming.

And that would be a good thing.

"Hello?"

"Hey, stranger, you okay?"

"Becca?"

"Yeah, I'm getting worried about you. I've only seen you once since the shower, and that was a month ago."

"I know. I'm sorry, Bec," Phyllis said, sinking

back in her chair with a grin. A good dose of Becca was just what she needed. "It's been a busy semester, but that's no excuse. I've missed you."

"We miss you, too. Bethany's growing so fast you aren't going to recognize her. She's got all four bottom teeth and two top ones."

Ouch. Phyllis cringed for her honorary niece. "She's had a tough month."

"Yeah, but we all survived. So, how was Thanksgiving at the Montfords'?" Becca asked.

"Great. I didn't stay that long." She'd been too sick, had spent most of the day between her bathroom and her bed. "Cassie's sure happy, though. It was great to see her in the center of such an adoring family."

"It's about time."

Polishing the base of the phone with her forefinger, Phyllis said, "For Sam and Mariah, too, I'd say."

They spent a few more minutes talking about their mutual friends. And then...

"So, how are you *really?*" Becca asked.

"Fine."

"You're sure?"

"Positive. Just really busy."

"Will and I were wondering if you'd like to come here for Christmas dinner. We're having his family over around one and we just won't be complete if you don't join us."

Everyone in this town was so sweet to her. She

might live alone, but she wasn't without family. On the contrary, she had several families from which to choose.

"Actually," she said slowly, "I'm having a couple of people over here for Christmas."

"You are?" Becca sounded surprised, but not unhappy. "Who? Tory and Ben? I thought they were going to the Montfords'."

"They are." Phyllis nodded her head, although no one was there to see. "They invited me along, too."

"So who's coming to your place?"

"Matt Sheffield, for one. You know him?"

"Know *of* him is more like it," Becca said, sounding impressed. "I've invited that man over more times than I can count in the four years he's been in town. How'd you manage to actually get him to say yes?"

"I've been talking with one of his students for him—a girl who's a bit troubled. She's staying in town for Christmas and we're having her over."

"Okay, then, but we'll still see you sometime during the holiday, right?" Becca asked. "We have to exchange our gifts."

"Of course we'll get together," Phyllis said. "I'll give you a call over the weekend."

"And you'll be coming to the annual holiday open house, right?" Becca asked. "I'm really glad we moved it from Christmas to New Year's. So many more people can come."

"Yeah, I'll be there," Phyllis said, remembering

last year's party, how warm and full she'd felt, being accepted and included in the families of Shelter Valley. She'd spent much of the time playing with Bethany, who'd been just under six months old. And worrying about Tory and Ben—who'd canceled at the last minute when Ben was suddenly granted complete custody of Alex.

Warmed by her friend's obvious caring, Phyllis decided it was time to tell Becca and everyone else about the babies. She was three and a half months along—had made it through the first trimester and gone almost two weeks without bleeding.

And when they asked who the father was?

She'd just have to—

The doorbell rang.

CHAPTER SEVENTEEN

PHYLLIS KNEW WHO was there. Heart pounding, she sat in her chair and tried to wipe the memory of the last five minutes of Matt's visit the previous night from her mind. Like an idiot she'd kissed him. Full on the mouth.

And it hadn't been a consoling kiss, or a friendly kiss, she thought, heading for the door when the bell rang a second time. This kiss had been hot and hungry. Like the kisses in the sound booth that day in September. The kisses that had led to the babies she was now carrying inside her.

But she and Matt were older now than they'd been three months before. Older and wiser. They'd broken off last night's kiss simultaneously and then, as if by mutual consent, he'd left before either of them could say anything about it.

Surely they could put it behind them...

Pulling open her door, she schooled her face into what she hoped was a noncommittal smile. "Hi, come on in," she said just as she had almost every night for the past two weeks. Tonight, though, instead of meeting his eyes, she looked past his left shoulder. Still, she was proud of how normal she sounded. Even if she *felt* anything but.

"Have a good day?" Matt asked, striding by her and into the kitchen to collect the trash. He didn't look at her, either.

Ugh.

"Yeah." As usual, she followed him. "You?"

"Fine." He pulled out a fresh garbage bag and lined her kitchen waste container before taking the partially full bag around the house to the various containers in other rooms. "Sophie's really glad to be joining us for Christmas dinner," he said when he returned to the kitchen, twisting the bag and securing it with a tie.

"Good."

He went out back to deposit the bag. He still hadn't looked at her.

She'd looked at him, though. A huge mistake.

He was wearing his maroon leather jacket. It was her favorite because of the way it came in tight at his waist. And the jeans he wore had not only seen many washings but knew just how to mold themselves to his tight butt.

Must be pregnancy hormones that were making her insides quake. Phyllis had learned to control her emotions long ago.

"I noticed a big box in the nursery," he said, entering the house, locking the back door behind him.

"Christmas presents I ordered through the Internet."

"Tell me you didn't carry it in there."

"I didn't." She was staring over his shoulder again. "I was here when they delivered it, and the guy was nice enough to carry it back for me."

"So, you need help getting it unpacked?" He stood in a familiar position, his fingers tucked into the front pockets of his jeans.

Phyllis usually noticed the fingers. Tonight she couldn't tear her eyes from the bulge they accentuated as they pulled the fabric taut.

"Maybe just opened," she said.

She had to get rid of him. Before she did something she'd really regret. Like beg him to stay. To join her in the bedroom. Or on the couch. Or even the floor.

Taking a knife from the kitchen, Matt went back to the spare room, which was now almost empty. He had the box open in no time and each of the packages out and lying neatly on top of the dresser that was still in the room.

They were mostly toys for Bethany. And Alex and Mariah.

"We're going to have to talk about it."

Phyllis's gaze flew to Matt's. His words had startled her. Panicked her.

"Can't we just pretend it never happened?"

He held her gaze, his far more steady and sure than hers. "I don't know," he said. "Can *you* do that?"

Phyllis looked away. She couldn't stand there, catching glimpses of the man inside him, and lie.

"I can't, either," he said.

The words were too soft, too unlike him, for her comfort.

"Should we, um, go in the living room?" she asked. She wasn't sure she wanted to return to the scene of the crime, but she had to sit down. He nodded and followed her there.

Phyllis sank into an armchair as soon as they reached the room.

Matt paced in front of her for a moment then sat on the edge of the couch, facing her. His knees were spread, his forearms on his thighs. His face, though lined with what looked like concentration, seemed more peaceful somehow.

Her stomach tensed. Her neck tensed. For the first time in more than a week, she felt as if she was going to throw up.

"I've been doing a lot of thinking since last night."

Phyllis merely nodded.

"You've given me a whole new way of looking at certain events in my life, a new understanding...."

"You're a good man, Matt Sheffield, one who deserves a full and complete life."

"It's going to take more than a day or two to change almost nine years of conditioning, but the thing is, I can't escape the possibility that you may be right. That with hard work and awareness, I may be able to have more of a life than I'd envisioned."

Tears sprang to Phyllis's eyes. Every bit of discomfort she'd put herself through last night—every night since she'd met him—was worth those two sentences he'd just uttered. "I'm glad," she told him. "So glad."

"And the logical conclusion following the first is that maybe I've found that life. Or it's found me."

Her breath caught in her throat.

"Oh?" she said when she was able to.

"Look at us, Phyllis," he said, warming to his subject—and scaring her to death. She'd been afraid *us* was what he'd meant by finding his life. "We not only get along well, we work together well. We enjoy each other's company. After all these weeks of living in each other's pockets, we haven't gotten tired of each other. And we have two children on the way. That's no small thing."

Not much of a declaration of undying love, but the words meant more to Phyllis than any declaration would have.

Which made it that much harder to shake her head. "I'm not in the market for either a relationship or a father for these babies."

"We're attracted to each other."

He had her there.

"Very attracted," he said, leaning forward to grab her hand and pull her onto the couch with him.

Phyllis was just needy enough to fall into those strong arms, lean against that gorgeous chest and turn her face up to welcome the kiss he was giving her. Her entire body quivered, her blood running hot through every vein in her body...and her belly filled with a much more insidious warmth.

God, she wanted him.

"Stop." She was so out of breath she wasn't sure how she got the words out. But she was grateful she had.

Matt's lips left hers, but he didn't let go of her.

"I can't." Phyllis pulled out of his arms, put some distance between them, one cushion's length.

"I've been meaning to ask you about that," Matt said, apparently not perturbed that she'd just rejected his lovemaking.

She wasn't sure she appreciated being so easily forgotten. And yet she was so immensely relieved she felt like crying.

"About what?"

"We both know why I wasn't interested in a relationship, even after we'd discovered that we made fantastic love and had a baby on the way, but we've never really talked about you—why an intelligent, beautiful, loving woman would want to live her life all alone."

"I'm not alone."

"You live alone."

"Only for five and a half more months."

"That's not what I mean. You're such a caring person, Phyllis. How can you be happy having no one?"

Phyllis grew completely still. The air around her seemed to freeze, encasing her. "I have someone."

His black eyes were bright, intense, as he leaned forward. "I'm not talking about the babies."

"Neither am I." She held his gaze, feeling defensive and not knowing why.

"You're alone in the ways that count, just as I've been alone for the past seven years."

She shook her head, still cold, still tense. Closing down. Shutting herself in. Familiar territory. Safe.

"Don't project your own emotions onto me, Matt. That's not how it works."

"So tell me, who shares your life with you?"

"Half this town!" Shelter Valley, the people here, had been a godsend to her, helping her through the pain of Christine's death, giving her a new life. "I have more friends than I know what to do with," she told him, remembering Becca's earlier call. Her second invitation to Christmas dinner.

Because he'd held himself apart from Shelter Valley's people, he had no idea what this town was made of, what belonging to this community could do.

"You know," he said, frowning, "maybe it's because I've been alone so much these past few years, but I've spent a lot of time watching people. You'd be surprised what you can learn if you have nothing invested, nothing to risk."

"Actually I wouldn't be," Phyllis said. "I've been watching people my entire life, even before I developed an interest in psychology."

"So, can I tell you what I see when I look at you?" he asked.

No. She slipped a little further inside, barricaded herself. "I guess, since I analyzed *you* last night, it's only fair that I hear you out," she said faintly.

"You helped me."

"And now you're ready to jump into the fray?"

She knew they'd been breaking down his walls these past weeks—but she hadn't expected such a quick and thorough razing.

"No," he told her. Somehow, with his denial, he gave her more confidence in his sudden reversal. "I have no idea how much—or how little—I'm going to be capable of," he said. "All I know is that I don't necessarily have to dismiss the notion of a future different from the one I expected. And because I have two children on the way—children I'm finding it difficult to turn my back on—I also find myself exploring the possibility that I might have fallen in love with their mother."

Phyllis choked.

And then started to cry, quiet, painful tears.

Matt watched her, his eyes narrowed. But nothing she did seemed to put him off.

"What I see when I look at you is a woman who was so badly hurt by something that she's in hiding."

"How can you *say* that?" Phyllis cried, anger her only defense at the moment. "I'm the one with all the friends!"

"Yes. There's safety in numbers."

"What do you mean by that?"

"Think about it, Phyllis. You don't have to share your life with anyone because no one knows *all* of you. You flit from one person to the next, giving this here and that there, and everyone's happy thinking that if you aren't with them, you're with someone else."

"That's because I usually am."

"Except when you're by yourself."

She watched him warily.

"And that's what you do whenever you're hurting, isn't it?" he asked softly. "That's the real reason you didn't want to tell everyone you were pregnant. Because you were frightened and in pain and you had to handle that on your own, deal with the confusion and uncertainty before you shared the news with the very people who should've been there to support you through it."

"They have their own problems to worry about, families and kids and lives."

"Exactly," Matt said, his eyes filled with an emotion she couldn't describe. It wasn't pity. And it wasn't simply caring, either. "You're always on the outside looking in. And what I really want to know is *why*?"

On the outside looking in. How dared he? This man who'd rejoined the living less than twenty four hours ago was suddenly the expert?

Phyllis closed her eyes. Searching for the perfect

rebuttal, the logical conclusion, so she could throw it at him and shut him up.

Except that, instead of finding the logical conclusion she expected, instead of voicing the rebuttal she'd planned, she started to shake.

"Maybe it's because I'm not all that lovable." The words hurt so much she could barely say them. "Simply by being myself, doing what I can't help doing. I...seem to intimidate people," she continued slowly, staring at the Christmas tree that had brought such hope the night before. "And since my ability to understand people, to see what they need, sense what they need, sometimes even before they do, isn't something I can change or control, I control what I can. My environment."

"If you don't get close enough to people, don't spend too much time with any one person, you don't have to worry about any of them deciding they can't stand to be around you."

Sounded pretty damn pathetic and sad to her. It also sounded exactly right.

"I guess."

"Can I pose another theory?"

"Of course." Not that she hadn't already been around and around this thing a hundred times herself. But he really was the sweetest man. Sensitive and strong...and still there.

"I think maybe you just hadn't met the right people yet when you felt rejected for having gifts that can heal hearts and minds and lives."

They were pretty words. She continued to stare at the tree, discovering that if she allowed her vision to blur just a little, the colored lights all flowed together and formed a rainbow.

"I suppose, if someone's insecure or, worse, being dishonest with you, having his head examined all the time would be a drag."

She could hardly see the ornaments now, only rows of rainbows.

"But a smart man, or woman, is going to welcome your talents, Phyllis. Smart people understand how lucky they are to have such great values in their lives. You make people happier with your help—it's that simple. How could any reasonably intelligent person turn that down?"

Rows and rows of rainbows. Swimming rainbows. Floating in a sea of tears.

"CAN I ASK JUST ONE more thing?" Matt broke the silence a few minutes later. He'd started to think Phyllis wasn't going to say anything at all, ever. He felt pretty certain he was correct where she was concerned, but had no idea how a guy like him reached a psychologist who knew everything he knew—and so much more.

"Yeah."

"Who is it that hurt you so badly?"

"There wasn't just one person. I wouldn't make life decisions based on a single incident, but rather on a series of them."

"So this series of incidents, they were all with men?"

"Every one of them."

"Guys you dated in college?" He pictured the cocky college boys he'd known.

"Most of them."

Could easily see them being too self-absorbed to know what a gift they'd had in Phyllis.

"You said you'd been married. How long ago was that?"

"A few years."

Matt didn't like to think of her married to another man. Loving another man. But she must've loved him. A lot. To have given him the power to hurt her this much.

"And how long were you married?"

"Four years."

"So what happened?"

"Brad thought I was a know-it-all. Couldn't stand how I always had the answers, as he put it. It got to the point where he never heard a word I said. Never really even listened to me when we talked. He heard what he *thought* I was going to say and nothing else."

"Sounds like a great guy."

"It wasn't completely his fault, you know," Phyllis said quietly.

Attacked by a pang he hardly recognized, Matt had to wonder if Phyllis was still in love with her ex-husband.

"And why is that?"

"Brad had to quit listening to me or lose himself. He quit listening to protect himself. I didn't mean to, but I made him feel stupid, insecure, unsure. And in retaliation, he was always trying to *educate* me," she said with a hint of bitterness. "Holding forth on political theory or the Industrial Revolution or Manifest Destiny—or whatever. Because it made him feel smarter than me."

What the guy deserved to feel was stupid, Matt thought but didn't say. Brad *was* stupid, and a jerk besides.

"So which one of you finally decided you'd had enough?" he asked, instead. Not that it mattered. She might still be in love with this Brad, even if she'd been the one to leave.

She laughed, a brittle laugh, still watching the tree that had been holding her attention for the past half hour. "It wasn't as straightforward as that."

"What happened?"

"Brad eventually grew so insecure that he turned to another woman. I caught him with her."

"He had an affair."

"More than one from what I understand."

Damn. He could imagine what that had done to Phyllis.

"You know that was because of a weakness in him, don't you? Not because of anything to do with you."

She finally turned her eyes on him, and Matt almost wished she hadn't. The sadness there was painful to see. And worse, he wasn't sure he could make it go away.

"Logically I know that," she said. "But I still have to wonder—if I'd been different, would I have been able to hold his interest?"

"Not if he was too shallow to know what a treasure he had in you."

Tears filled her eyes again and Matt wanted to reach over and wipe them away.

"Look at what you do, Phyllis, what a great gift you have. Your friend Tory is just one example. You helped a woman who was on a fast course to hell, and she's now a happily married woman, and a mother with a loving extended family."

"Tory did most of that herself. I just listened."

"And counseled."

"Maybe."

After a lifetime of being alone, Matt didn't really know how to open up, but he owed it to her to try.

"Look what you've done for me," he said, imbued with an unfamiliar and powerful emotion. "When I first met you, I hated myself so much I could hardly look other people in the eye...because I had to spare them what I saw as my tainted presence." He held her gaze steadily, but the effort it took cost him. "Somehow, without my even realizing it, you gave me back a sense of worth I didn't know I possessed. You found value in me, and through you I'm now beginning to find it in myself."

"Anybody you'd let close enough could have done the same."

"But you," he said, nodding toward her once, "you were able to meet me where I was and bring me out to where *you* were. And I *know* that not just anyone could've done that. It took someone with special vision, Phyllis. Someone who could see something I couldn't see myself."

She watched him silently for several long minutes, obviously assessing everything he'd said.

"Where did you come from, Matt Sheffield?" she whispered at last, a tremulous smile hovering on her lips.

"I don't know," he told her a bit hoarsely. "But I'm glad I ended up here."

Leaning forward, her elbows on her knees, Phyllis laid her head sideways on her hands, looking over at him. "It would appear that we're a pretty sorry pair."

"But a matching one."

"I can't make any promises."

"Which is a good thing, because until I know whether or not I have enough trust left inside me to build on, I can't accept any."

"Is that enough of an understanding to take me to bed?"

"I thought you'd never ask...."

CHAPTER EIGHTEEN

PHYLLIS WAS UP making breakfast the next morning while Matt showered. They both had to be on campus early for a meeting, but he still had to drive out to his place to change. She'd already showered and was proudly wearing a black skirt she'd had to pin closed beneath the matching red-and-black jacket.

The oatmeal and toast were ready at about the time she heard the water shut off. And while she'd like to have stood there daydreaming, recalling what Matt looked like, imagining that gorgeous body dripping wet from the shower, she had to decide where to put his bowl of oatmeal, instead.

Setting a place at the table seemed like such a commitment. Yet didn't leaving his bowl on the counter, where he usually ate, mean they were taking a step backward?

Unable to make a decision and hating the fact that she was thrown off course by such an inconsequential thing, Phyllis finally left the bowl empty by the pan of oatmeal.

Let him decide.

With damp hair, but completely dressed, including

his leather lace-up shoes, Matt joined her in the kitchen.

Her heart leapt, just looking at him. Out of incredible desire. And an equal measure of fear. Could she do this? Could she really allow herself to believe to that this man wanted her?

How could she trust that much?

How could she not?

"There's oatmeal…"

"I don't normally eat breakfast." He glanced at her, and she could see the desire, banked but still glowing, in his eyes. Yet there was uncertainty, as well as satisfaction in his demeanor. She could read it in the way he was rocking, almost imperceptibly, back and forth on his feet. The tension in his hands. The brevity of his gaze.

"I didn't, either, until I was eating for three," she said.

He grinned at her. At least the babies were something certain between them. "Then you'd best get to feeding them before they start to complain," he said.

Phyllis nodded, grateful to have something to do as she filled a bowl, buttered a piece of toast and, in bare feet, crossed the room to her usual place at the table.

"Will's going to be taking a final count at the meeting this morning of all the faculty planning to attend his New Year's Eve party," she said. She'd been planning to go—she'd gone the previous year, when it was still an annual Christmas open house, and she'd had a great time—but suddenly wondered about the protocol of things here. Did they go as a couple? *Were* they a couple?

Or did she just go alone, as usual?

This was all so awkward. So complicated and confusing.

"Seems to me that would be a good time to come out—so to speak," he said, still rocking. His eyes were jumping from one object to another in her kitchen. "You won't be able to hide your pregnancy much longer...."

"I'd already decided to tell everyone."

He looked directly at her. "But the telling's going to be different now, isn't it?" His gaze was steady now, calming her just a bit. "Those babies have a father."

Something lifted inside Phyllis. A weight she hadn't known was there. "They always did have."

He was still watching her. "We're in this together, then. The New Year's Eve party would be as good a time as any to get everybody used to that fact."

Phyllis nodded.

Grabbing his keys from the pocket of his jacket, Matt moved toward the hall that would take him to the front of the house. "Kind of fitting, in a way," he said, standing there with one foot in the kitchen, one in the hall. "New Year's Eve—time of new beginnings."

And with that—and no kiss—he was gone.

Phyllis wondered which of them was more relieved.

IT WAS SATURDAY afternoon, three days before Christmas and two days since Matt had spent the night at her house. Although he'd been over the day before, there'd been no repeat performance of that incredible lovemaking. But they'd talked. About their pasts. And about the future they both wanted, but weren't sure they could trust.

"Hey, Tor, it's Phyllis. Got a minute?"

Perched on the edge of her bed, Phyllis twirled the phone cord around her index finger.

"Of course," Tory said. "Chrissie's asleep, Ben and Sam are out shopping—last-minute, typical-male style—and Carol drove down to the diner to pick up some lunch. Alex went with her."

Phyllis had to grin. It felt so damn good to hear the happiness in Tory's voice. The perfect family scenario she'd described. Ben Sanders and Sam Montford were cousins, joint heirs to the Montford fortune, who'd only found each other within the past year.

"Carol's still coming over everyday?" Phyllis asked. As neither Tory nor Ben had living parents, Sam's mom, Carol—Ben's aunt—had taken over the role of mother to Tory and Ben, too.

"Yes," Tory said, but although she tried to sound exasperated, her tone was filled with wonder. And love. "I got my stitches out four days ago, but she still insists I shouldn't be left alone."

"She's a very special person," Phyllis said, wishing she could hug Carol right then and there. Phyllis might be able to help people think through their problems, but Carol Montford was the real healer among them.

"I know," Tory said, her voice as quiet as it used to be when Phyllis had first met her. "I can't believe I'm so lucky."

"After the first twenty-three years you survived, you deserve every ounce of luck that comes your way," Phyllis assured her friend. "Let yourself believe in it, soak it up, and it'll keep right on coming."

Tory chuckled. "You're very good for me, you know that?"

"Am I, Tor?"

"Of course! What's up?"

Phyllis heard the immediate concern in Tory's voice. She obviously hadn't hidden her doubts as well as she'd intended. But then Tory was the one person in Shelter Valley who'd seen Phyllis at her worst. Fat and miserable and in mourning for her best friend. Because Tory had been living with her, Phyllis had been unable to conceal her emotions from the younger woman.

"Do you think I hide behind my friendships?"

"I'm assuming you want honesty here," Tory said slowly. "Like before you lost the weight and you wanted me to tell you the truth about how you looked and what we had to do to fix it.''

Locking her knees, feet braced against the floor, Phyllis said, ''Just like then.''

''Maybe you do hide a little,'' Tory said in a rush, then continued, ''But who wouldn't, Phyllis? You've had rotten luck with men, an even worse marriage, and then, when you finally have a best friend, she dies....'' Tory's voice broke on the last word.

Both women were silent for an emotional moment, sharing the pain they would always share at the memory of Christine.

''But do I hide from you guys, too? Put up barriers when I might be the one who needs help?''

''Most definitely.''

No softening the blow on that one. Not that Phyllis was really surprised by the answer. She'd been doing a lot of thinking this past couple of days. Matt had revealed something important to her, something she'd refused to see. The clarity of vision she habitually brought to the problems of others she now brought to her own.

''I've always thought that you keep yourself busy helping everyone else so that you won't have time to see what's going on inside you,'' Tory said, her words, though harsh, brimming with love.

''I was digging myself into a hole and didn't even notice the dirt closing in around me,'' Phyllis said, half to herself. She studied the paint on the wall, the texturing, looking for a pattern that wasn't completely random. "I really believed that my life was finally perfect."

Tory laughed—a rich sound that delighted Phyllis, who recalled a time when Tory didn't laugh at all. Or even smile. "And this from a psychologist?" she asked. "You of all people know that life isn't *ever* perfect. Like you've taught me, there'll always be trials. But happiness comes when we can create a solid base of security and love for ourselves. That's what sees us through those trials."

"Physician, heal thyself, huh?" Phyllis said, chuckling a little, too.

"Is that what you're doing, Phyl? Healing?"

Phyllis continued to glance from one swirl of paint to the next, looking for anything that repeated itself, giving even a hint of organization.

And she thought about Matt, remembering the expression on his face when he'd sat in front of her Christmas tree the night before, with only the colored lights illuminating the room—and him—as he told her how much he'd always hated Christmas.

"I don't know," she answered her friend. "I just know I have to try...."

THAT EVENING, after doing a couple of chores for her, Matt took Phyllis to see his house. She hadn't asked his permission, but she'd brought along some Christmas decorations to put up while she was there. Somehow she knew she had to teach this man to believe in Christmas if they were to have any chance at a life together.

She'd dressed festively for the occasion, as well— black leggings, a long chenille sweater boldly red to show off her hair and black leather boots with just enough of a heel to be sassy. And sexy.

Although it probably wasn't the most mature idea she'd ever had, she was hoping they were going to christen Matt's home with more than just decorations.

"What's in there?" he asked, glancing at the big black plastic trash bag she'd carried to the car.

Phyllis grinned at him. "A surprise," was all she said. She refused to give him a chance to tell her no. She knew he needed this, even if he didn't.

He was wearing black jeans and a forest-green, button-down corduroy shirt underneath his black leather jacket. His hair was mussed and inviting. And staring at him, Phyllis got the shock of her life.

She was in love with him.

She loved Matt Sheffield. Totally. Completely. As much as she loved the babies growing inside her.

"What's wrong?" he asked, his brow creased with concern.

"Um, nothing," she said, turning to look out the window. "Is it much farther?"

"A couple of miles," he said, slowing the Blazer. "You feeling sick again?"

She was. But not the way he meant. She hadn't

had a bout of morning sickness that week. She shook her head.

And forced herself to concentrate on the log house as it came into view. Taking in the burnished wood, the fieldstone foundation, the sparkling windows. Knowing as she did, that Matt had helped build the place with his own two hands.

She hadn't meant to be impressed, but she was. His home was beautiful.

They went inside. "One thing's for sure," she said, looking around, admiring the polished hardwood floors and perfectly chosen trim, the wet bar by the fireplace, the state-of-the-art kitchen. "If we ever do end up living together, it's not going to be at my place."

She wished she'd bitten her tongue. That statement had been far too presumptuous.

"In town would be more convenient," he said, not missing a beat as he poured her a glass of orange juice. "And much closer to school when the time comes."

He bent to turn on the gas fireplace.

Phyllis gulped her drink.

Maybe they really *were* thinking of a future. Making plans. Even if those plans were so tentative neither of them could make a commitment yet.

And then, setting down her glass, she dipped into the bag she'd brought. A wreath for his door. A one-and-a-half-foot-tall ceramic Christmas tree that had little colored bulbs in tiny holes all around it. They lit up when the tree was plugged in, and the effect was both simple and charming. A cross-stitch of a couple of kids peering over the banister at their tree on Christmas Eve, with the words, "'Twas the Night before Christmas" embroidered across the top. It was something her mother had made and given her years before; Phyllis took pleasure in sharing it with Matt.

"What are you doing?" he asked, turning around to find her delving in her bag.

"This is your first Christmas, Matt," she said, trying to instill equal amounts of cheer and determination in her voice. She wasn't going to surrender on this one. "We can't let it happen without getting your home ready for it."

With a hammer and nail she'd brought from home—so she wouldn't have to ask Matt—she grabbed the cross-stitch and headed for a patch of wall beside the fireplace. Every muscle in her body was tense, ready to wrestle him for the wall—and the seconds it would take her to mar it with her gift.

She marched right up to the wall. Took a visual measure, hammered, hung the cross-stitched kids, smiling at the wonder and anticipation shining in their eyes. Then she straightened it and stepped back.

He hadn't tried to stop her.

As a matter-of-fact, he hadn't argued at all. He'd remained completely silent.

With renewed courage and a lot of curiosity, Phyllis turned, half-expecting to find that he'd walked out on her.

He was standing in the middle of the room, studying the picture she'd just hung.

He opened his mouth and Phyllis braced herself for the argument she'd rehearsed.

"Thank you."

They were the sweetest words she'd ever heard.

A COUPLE OF HOURS LATER, feeling the glow from their joint decorating escapade—and the joint lovemaking adventure that followed—Phyllis wandered into Matt's kitchen looking for him. When she'd gone into the bathroom to shower, he'd said he was going to get some dinner started for them.

He was grilling steaks on the back porch. Baked potatoes were in the oven—the kind that came frozen and stuffed from the grocery store—and a loaf of French bread sat on the counter. The table was set with earthenware china and matching stainless-steel cutlery, as well as a large wooden salad bowl heaped with romaine lettuce, sliced tomatoes and avocado.

For someone who'd never known a real home, Matt had sure done a spectacular job of making one for himself.

There were a couple of letters on the counter waiting to be mailed. For some reason, that touch of normal, everyday life gave Phyllis more security than the immaculately set table.

As she walked by the counter on her way to the

back door, a name on the first envelope caught her attention. Probably because it was handwritten and she wasn't familiar enough with Matt's handwriting not to be curious about it.

Once she saw the name, however, the handwriting didn't matter.

What on earth was Matt mailing to Shelley Monroe? What could he possibly have to say to a girl who'd let him lose two years of his life sitting in a prison cell?

She picked up the envelope, intending to ask him about it, then abruptly put it back down. She recognized what had been clearly visible through the thin white envelope.

A check.

Matt was sending Shelley Monroe money.

"She's only twenty-three years old."

She hadn't heard him come in. But when she swung toward him, she could tell that he knew he should have told her.

Phyllis's heart sank. She wasn't surprised. Not even a little bit. He didn't trust her, not completely. Not enough to tell her something this important. She knew the feeling well. Her ex-husband had held out on her, too.

"She has a nine-year-old son and she's trying to get a college education so she can give him one."

"You don't have to justify yourself to me."

"I've been sending her money since the beginning…"

"Must've made it harder for the jury to believe you when you said you weren't guilty."

He shrugged. "Maybe, but I couldn't let that stop me from being responsible for my actions."

"You didn't sleep with her. The child isn't yours. You have no responsibility."

"I led her on. I encouraged a fourteen-year-old kid to think of herself as a desirable woman."

"Someday."

His eyes were piercing when she finally looked at him again. "She missed that part," he said.

"It's not the money that matters, anyway," Phyllis told him honestly. Her stomach was churning. She didn't know if she should go out and get some fresh air or prepare to make a dash for the bathroom.

Matt, coming up behind her, took hold of her shoulders, gently turning her to face him. "What, then?"

Although Phyllis struggled against her tears, she didn't quite succeed.

"The fact that you didn't trust me enough to tell me about the 'guilt' payments," she told him. "You didn't want to hear what I thought of them."

"I—"

"It's okay, Matt," she said, pulling away from him. She'd left her purse in the living room, hadn't she? Next to the trash bag they'd emptied. "Brad and the couple of guys I was serious about before him couldn't give themselves wholly to me, either. They were afraid of what I'd do with the things I learned about them. Or more accurately, what I might try to make them feel.''

''You've got it wrong this time.'' Matt sounded just sure enough to make her turn around.

His gaze was forthright, completely open. And so understanding.

''How's that?'' she asked.

''I did deliberately withhold the information,'' he admitted, and her heart, which had picked up hope, dropped it again. ''But not for the reason you assume.''

She was still listening, trying to suspend judgment long enough to hear what he had to say. Still listening because she couldn't do anything else.

''I didn't tell you because I was afraid that if you knew, you'd assume just what the jury assumed—that if I was paying her, I must be guilty of the claims she'd made.''

Phyllis stood there for a full minute, digesting what he'd said, replaying his explanation in her mind, analyzing it from every angle. Tone of voice. Body posture. Content.

He was telling her the truth. And it was about trust. About being afraid to trust. Not about her at all.

With tears in her eyes, she wrapped her arms around him, pressing her head to his chest, absorbing the reassuring beat of his heart. ''Please,'' she said against his shirt, ''please don't ever keep things from me again. *Trust me.*''

Matt lifted her head with gentle fingers, holding her face up to his. "And you're going to trust me, too?" he asked.

Trust him to tell her the truth? Or trust him not to leave her like all the others? Trust him to love her for who she was?

Phyllis might have been able to give him the answer he wanted if he'd even once said he loved her.

HIS FIRST CHRISTMAS was turning out to be far more than he'd ever imagined. Because in all the movies he'd ever seen, the TV shows, the windows he'd peeked into as a kid, he'd seen only the trappings of Christmas, lovely as those were. He'd never known that what made Christmas wasn't the food, or the presents, the decorations or the colorful lights. It was the warmth, the ineffable sense of contentment, that pervaded the room, the house, the day.

He'd thought, during his years in Shelter Valley, that he'd found peace. On this first Christmas, during his thirty-fourth year of life, he finally discovered what the word meant.

"You know what's the absolute best thing about this day?" Sophie asked him quietly, leaning across the table while Phyllis mashed the potatoes at the stove.

"What?"

The kid looked great. Happy. Matt was glad Phyllis had invited her to join them.

"The fact that you want me to become friends

with your friends," she said, an odd gleam in her eyes.

Matt's radar went off, warning him of something very bad. His stomach tensed.

"Here we are." Phyllis sounded so happy that Matt felt happy, too, as she joined them, passing around turkey and dressing, mashed potatoes and gravy, rolls, broccoli and a seven-layer salad.

By the time the meal was finished, he'd almost forgotten the dread that had invaded the most perfect day he could ever remember.

He'd managed to convince himself that he'd overreacted. He didn't have to be so guarded anymore. The past was past. He'd proved himself here in Shelter Valley. More importantly, he'd proved himself *to* himself. He was a good man. A man worthy to be sitting at this table, enjoying the first real peace he'd ever known.

A man worthy enough to love the woman sitting across from him?

"Dessert?" Phyllis asked. "There's Dutch apple pie with vanilla ice cream, or homemade sugar cookies with confectioner's icing."

"I'd like both," Matt said, rubbing his already full belly. He just wasn't ready for the experience to end.

"Me, too," Sophie said.

Phyllis laughed. "How can either of you have room for two desserts?"

"I have a separate dessert compartment," Matt boasted.

Sophie laughed. Phyllis gave him a wicked wink. Matt's day was complete.

He only made it halfway through the two desserts, but he noticed Sophie still going to town on hers. His eyes met Phyllis's over the girl's head. *She's fine,* his tried to say. Phyllis shook her head, frowning.

And ten minutes later, he understood why. While Phyllis and Matt were busy with the dishes, Sophie excused herself and disappeared. Phyllis waited only a moment before grabbing his hand and following the girl.

"I hope I'm wrong," she whispered as they practically tiptoed down the hall to the guest bathroom.

She wasn't wrong. Sadness engulfed Matt as he listened to the sounds coming from inside that room. Sophie was ridding herself of all the food she'd just eaten.

Even he knew what that meant. Bulimia.

On such a good day, surrounded by people who were genuinely fond of her, people who believed in and supported her, with presents yet to open under the tree, Sophie couldn't just relax and give herself a break.

When she opened the door, Matt and Phyllis were still standing there.

"Sorry, I wasn't feeling well," she said, not looking either of them in the eye. "Must have eaten too much. But don't worry, I didn't make a mess or anything."

"I couldn't care less about that," Phyllis said. She wrapped an arm around the girl's shoulders and led her into the living room, sitting beside her on the couch. Not sure what he should do, Matt sat on Sophie's other side.

Support seemed important at that moment.

"You've got a problem, Sophie," Phyllis said bluntly. "Do you know much about eating disorders?"

The girl stiffened, but Matt noticed she didn't shrug off Phyllis's touch. "I don't have an eating disorder."

"Forcing yourself to regurgitate your dinner is an eating disorder."

"That's the first time I've ever done that."

"I don't believe you," Phyllis said. She wasn't giving the girl any leeway at all. Matt respected her for it. "Look at your finger. That sore on your knuckle testifies to how often—and how recently—you've been making yourself throw up."

Sophie slid both hands under her thighs.

Matt couldn't stand to see her suffering so much. She was a great kid. Had so much potential, if she'd just believe in herself.

"If you won't let me help you with this, I'm going to have to turn you over to a school counselor when school starts again," Phyllis said.

"You promised you wouldn't go to anybody with what we talked about!"

"All I have to tell a counselor is what happened here this afternoon."

Sophie didn't relent. Didn't admit to anything. Didn't do anything but sit there between them, her hands beneath her, staring at the Christmas tree.

"Why, Soph?" Matt couldn't keep quiet any longer. "Why are you doing this to yourself?"

He was shocked when she turned angry, tearful eyes on him. "How can you ask me that?" she demanded. "You should know why." She bowed her head.

He should?

He and Phyllis exchanged a glance, but he couldn't give her any answers. He was as puzzled as she was.

"It was all for you." The words were mumbled, her tone defeated. "I thought you knew that."

"For me?" Matt's heart started to pound. His lungs felt as if they were closing, depriving him of air.

She gazed at him, her eyes imploring. And he began to understand.

He was going to be sick.

"I know how you feel about me," she said. "And I know you think you have to give me lots of time because you're older than me. It makes me feel good that you're taking such care to do things right for us, that it means so much to you...."

Matt could hardly believe this was happening. He stared at his hands. At least they were familiar. He recognized them. He couldn't have looked at Phyllis if his life had depended on it.

"But the thing is," Sophie said, her voice growing more confident—so confident it frightened him, "I already feel the same way about you that you feel about me. I don't need the time. What I need to do is make sure that when you finally decide we can be together, my body's as perfect as any woman's you've ever been with. I won't have you thinking of me as a child. I'm going to be a *woman* for you."

As the life slowly faded out of Matt, Sophie turned to Phyllis.

"I'm sorry I'm saying all this in front of you," she said. "You shouldn't be dragged into our situation, but you know all about it, anyway, and I just can't keep quiet anymore."

"Matt's the man you were talking about, then?" Phyllis's voice sounded so unnatural Matt raised his eyes to her.

But only for the split second it took for her to look back at him, her expression clouded by doubt. He'd already been tried, convicted, sentenced.

Nine years ago.

And today.

It wasn't ever going to happen again.

He didn't wait around for whatever was going to happen next.

He'd already seen too much.

"MATT, WAIT!"

Phyllis was running after him, but Matt couldn't

stop. Get to the Blazer. Start the engine. Return to the reality he knew.

"Matt, I'm begging you!" She was crying as she chased him out to his truck. Crying and apparently determined. When he started the engine, she grabbed the door handle.

"Matt, don't do this!" Her voice was muffled through the closed door, but not muffled enough. He could still hear the pain.

A pain that echoed low in his gut and throughout the rest of him. Alone was so much better than this.

But he couldn't drive away with her hanging on to the car door.

"I love you, you idiot! Please listen to me."

The pain. The anger. The despair. It all just stopped. He was numb. Matt rolled down the window.

"What did you say?" He was staring straight ahead.

"I said I love you, and if you think for one second that I was doubting you back there, you'd better have a damn good apology for me. I'd suspected it was you she loved, but when she was so certain that the man loved her back, I'd dismissed my suspicion. Too quickly. And the only excuse I have is that I was too personally involved to be objective."

Matt had a feeling this wasn't a good time to smile. But he couldn't help it. The grin spread right across his face.

"You've never told me you loved me."

"You've never told me, either."

"Well, I do."

"I do, too."

He turned then, searching those beautiful green eyes for the truth he needed to find there. "You really do?"

"Yeah, I do."

"I love you, Phyllis," he said, grabbing her hand through the window to hold on to her while he slowly eased open the car door and pulled her onto his lap. "I think I have since that first day in the sound booth. I've never made love to a woman like that in my life."

"I never knew sex could be that...everything."

Matt absorbed her honesty—with gratitude and with anticipation. "You know what? Neither did I."

"Does this mean you're ready to trust me?"

"I already trusted you, I just didn't know it yet."

Her gaze was sweet and honest and direct, holding nothing back. "I trusted you, too," she whispered.

Matt took a deep breath, pondering the words he had to say next. "Enough to marry me?"

If she said no, life—as he wanted to believe it could be—was over before it could even begin.

"I thought you'd never ask."

They had much to discuss, confessing to do, love to make, but for now, his arm around Phyllis, they went back inside to the distraught young college student standing on Phyllis's front porch.

"Matt?" Sophie asked, her eyes locked on Matt's arm around Phyllis's waist.

"Let's go back inside," Matt said, throwing his free arm around Sophie's shoulders, giving her no choice but to comply.

He had no idea what came next but felt confident that together, he and Phyllis would figure it out.

SOPHIE WANTED TO DIE. Wished she was alone so she could do just that.

"How could you?" she yelled at Matt. At Dr. Langford. At *them*. "Why did you invite me here if you two were just going to go behind my back...and want each other?"

"I didn't realize we were going behind your back," Dr. Langford said softly. "I had no idea the man you'd told me about was Matt"

She stared at the floor, wishing she could shrug off the guards flanking her, but too needy for their touch to do so. "Well, *he* knew," she said in her meanest voice.

"Soph, you know I've never said or done anything that could lead you to believe I was interested in you romantically," Matt was saying, his arm still around her as she sat sandwiched between him and Dr. Langford on the couch. Dr. Langford was holding her hand.

Humiliation worse than she'd ever known crept up her skin, making her feel light-headed, hot. And suddenly nothing mattered. Nothing. Not Matt. Not her appearance. Not the past or the future. Nothing.

And with the freedom that nothingness offered, all the weight she'd been carrying, the pretense, slid off her shoulders. She didn't even care that she couldn't hold back the gross-sounding sobs, or that her face looked like crap with tears streaming down it.

"So all the praise was a lie," she said, her voice devoid of caring. "I'm nothing special. Not to you, not to anyone."

"Wrong." Matt's voice was forceful, more than she'd ever heard it. He squeezed her shoulder so tightly it almost hurt. "You *are* special. To me. But not romantically."

Sophie felt a little bit pathetic at being so easily appeased. After all, what else could he say, considering the predicament he was in?

"I can attest to that," Dr. Langford said, rubbing the top of Sophie's hand lightly. "Matt's spoken of you many times, told me how much you amaze him. He often talks about your artistic talent."

She didn't want to, but Sophie had to look at him then. "You do?"

He didn't even blink, just stared her straight in the eye and nodded.

And that was when Sophie really fell apart. When she had to admit to herself, and then to her hosts, that maybe she wasn't *really* in love with Matt. That what she needed was the belief that someone older and wiser, someone she respected, actually cared about her. Needed to think she had someone in the world she could turn to.

MATT SWALLOWED HARD as Sophie's sobbing voice choked out the thin thread of words that told of a lost lonely girl searching for something that should have been hers unconditionally. The love and guidance that all children required from the people who were supposed to be raising them.

After more than an hour of listening, Phyllis managed to get the girl to admit that she had an eating disorder. She persuaded Sophie to let them help her, to let them care. And to be her friends.

By the time Phyllis got around to telling Sophie that she was pregnant, Sophie was claiming an exclusive on baby-sitting rights. She seemed almost relieved to have Phyllis filling the womanly place in Matt's life, allowing Sophie to be a young adult, who could turn to him for guidance—no strings attached.

The day waned, and eventually they all made it back to the kitchen for seconds on dessert—which Sophie promised to hang on to this time. Matt couldn't help thinking it had taken only one Christmas for him to know instinctively what life was all about. Love and friendship. After thirty-four years of searching, he'd found both.

EPILOGUE

AT THREE O'CLOCK on New Year's Eve, in a chapel in Las Vegas, Matt Sheffield made Phyllis Langford his wife.

They didn't stay in the city long. Just long enough to use it for what they needed—a wedding ceremony that would bind them together forever.

And then they were on a plane back to Phoenix. They had a party to attend. Friends to face.

"Do you think they're going to be mad that we didn't invite them?" Matt asked. Her friends were all people he'd known longer than she had, but he knew none of them even half as well.

"Of course not," his wife assured him, beautiful in her white maternity suit, short red hair sassy as ever. Even after the tears she'd shed at their wedding, she looked impeccable. "Now that they'll finally get to know you, they're going to love you, Matt."

"But still, they might've wanted to be included..."

He didn't know why he was being such a damned idiot. He just knew that suddenly he had a lot to lose. Something he'd never had before.

"They'll only want me to be happy, Matt, and I

can vouch for you there. I'd never known what
happy was until I met you...."

A COUPLE OF HOURS LATER, Phyllis waited by the
front door of her house as Matt started the Blazer
and turned on the heat. They'd had cold weather
move in—it was a chilly thirty-five degrees—and
Phyllis no longer owned a winter coat.

Besides it would've seemed wrong to cover the
beautiful gown Matt and she had picked out at the
maternity store in Phoenix the day before. Rather
than concealing her condition, as most of her clothes
did, the black silk gown proclaimed it. Phyllis wore
it proudly.

Noticing the New Year's decorations on her front
door, she had to smile. Matt had put them there.
She'd teased him that she'd created a holiday mon-
ster. He was planning to decorate his house—which
would be their house as soon as they got her stuff
moved—for every holiday, including the Fourth of
July. And Thanksgiving. Mother's Day, of course...
and Father's Day.

"Your carriage awaits, my lady."

He'd returned, was standing on the other side of
the screen door, resplendent in his black evening
wear. But it was the little paper hat sitting jauntily
on his head, a hat with a pointed top, foil across the
bottom and string elastic stapled to each side that
split her heart wide open.

"Matt?" The word was barely a whisper.

"Yes, love?" He turned. Frowned. Pulled open

the door with far more force than necessary. "Is something wrong?"

"No!" She found her voice long enough to reassure him. "Just...could you tell me again why we got married today, and why we're telling everyone at the party tonight?"

She knew why. She just wanted to hear him say it again. Wanted to hear that reminder every day for the rest of her life.

"It's all about new beginnings," he told her. "Starting tonight, we enter a new month, a new year, a new life."

"You mean that," she said, searching those dark eyes for the peace she needed to find there. "The past is gone forever. For you. In your heart."

"It's in your keeping, Phyl," he said softly. "I gave it to you."

Leaning forward, she kissed him, a deep, familiar kiss. A kiss that promised him she'd keep the past, and anything else he gave her, in a safe place. A faraway place, where it could never touch him again.

"Can I ask you one more thing?" she said huskily.

"Of course."

"Would you mind terribly if you had to get into that outfit a second time?"

It was another hour before they finally left for the party.

The pointed hat with foil on the bottom dressed the pillow on their bed. It would wait there until they returned home again, to claim everything they'd found there.

HARLEQUIN *Super***ROMANCE**

Old friends, best friends...

Girlfriends

Your friends are an important part of your life. You confide in them, laugh with them, cry with them....

Girlfriends

Three new novels by Judith Bowen

Zoey Phillips. Charlotte Moore. Lydia Lane.
They've been best friends for ten years, ever since the summer they all worked together at a lodge. At their last reunion, they all accepted a challenge: *look up your first love.* Find out what happened to him, how he turned out....

Join Zoey, Charlotte and Lydia as they rediscover old loves and find new ones.

Read all the *Girlfriends* books! Watch for
Zoey Phillips in November, *Charlotte Moore* in
December and *Lydia Lane* in January.

HARLEQUIN®
Makes any time special ®

Two city gals are about to turn life upside
down for two Wyoming ranchers in

Cowboy Country

Two full-length novels of true
Western lovin' from favorite authors

JUDITH BOWEN
RENEE ROSZEL

Available in January 2002 at your favorite retail outlet.

HARLEQUIN®
Makes any time special ®

Harlequin Romance®
Love affairs that last a lifetime.

HARLEQUIN *Presents*
Seduction and passion guaranteed.

Harlequin® Historical
Historical Romantic Adventure.

HARLEQUIN *Temptation.*
Sassy, sexy, seductive!

HARLEQUIN *Superromance®*
Emotional, exciting, unexpected.

HARLEQUIN AMERICAN *Romance®*
Heart, home & happiness.

HARLEQUIN *Duets*™
Romantic comedy.

HARLEQUIN® INTRIGUE®
Breathtaking romantic suspense.

HARLEQUIN® *Blaze*™
Red-Hot Reads.

HARLEQUIN®
Makes any time special®

*Together for the first time
in one Collector's Edition!*

New York Times bestselling authors

Barbara Delinsky

Catherine Coulter

Linda Howard

Forever Yours

**A special trade-size volume containing three
complete novels that showcase the passion,
imagination and stunning power that these
talented authors are famous for.**

Coming to your favorite retail outlet in December 2001.

HARLEQUIN®
Makes any time special ®

Visit us at www.eHarlequin.com

PHFY